'Please, I didn't mean to annoy you. It's just—well, I'm sure there are places you'd much rather be than here.'

'And if there are not?'

Her tongue appeared between her teeth and he felt the sudden tightness in his loins as she wet her lips. 'You're sure you're not just saying that?'

'No.' He hunkered down beside her, one hand moving of its own accord to cup her cheek. He tilted her face to his. 'Believe me, *cara,* at this moment there is no place I would rather be than here.' His eyes darkened as they rested on her mouth. But only for a second. He was on dangerous ground, he realised, aware of what he really wanted to do. Withdrawing his hand abruptly, he got to his feet again, looking down at her. *'Bene,'* he said tensely. 'Enjoy the rest of your meal. I will not be long.'

D0599785

New York Times bestselling author **Anne Mather** has written since she was seven, but it was only when her first child was born that she fulfilled her dream of becoming a writer. Her first book, CAROLINE, appeared in 1966. It met with immediate success, and since then Anne has written more than 140 novels, reaching a readership which spans the world.

Born and raised in the north of England, Anne still makes her home there, with her husband, two children and, now, grandchildren. Asked if she finds writing a lonely occupation, she replies that her characters always keep her company. In fact, she is so busy sorting out their lives that she often doesn't have time for her own! An avid reader herself, she devours everything from sagas and romances to mainstream fiction and suspense. Anne has also written a number of mainstream novels, with DANGEROUS TEMPTATION, her most recent title, published by MIRA® Books.

Recent titles by the same author:

THE RODRIGUES PREGNANCY
SINFUL TRUTHS
ALEJANDRO'S REVENGE

IN THE ITALIAN'S BED

BY
ANNE MATHER

MILLS & BOON®

First published in Great Britain 2004
Harlequin Mills & Boon Limited,
Eton House, 18-24 Paradise Road, Richmond, Surrey TW9 1SR

© Anne Mather 2004

ISBN 0 263 83752 1

Set in Times Roman 10½ on 11 pt.
01-0704-56853

Printed and bound in Spain
by Litografia Rosés, S.A., Barcelona

CHAPTER ONE

THE man was standing outside the Medici Gallery as Tess drove past. She only caught a brief glimpse of him, concentrating as she was on keeping Ashley's car on the right side of the road. She saw him look after her as she turned into the parking lot behind the smart row of boutiques and cafés that faced the flower-fringed promenade of Porto San Michele. And wondered if she wasn't being paranoid in imagining there had been a definite air of hostility in his gaze.

She shook off the thought impatiently. She was imagining things. He wasn't waiting for her. Besides, she wasn't late. Well, only a few minutes anyway. She doubted Ashley's timekeeping was any better than hers.

There were few cars in the parking lot at this hour of the morning. Tess had discovered that Italian shops rarely opened before ten and were definitely disposed towards a leisurely schedule. Her neighbours on the parade—Ashley's neighbours, actually—seldom kept to strict opening hours. But they were charming and helpful, and Tess had been grateful for their advice in the three days since she'd been standing in for Ashley.

She hoped she was mistaken about the man, she thought as she let herself into the gallery through the back entrance. She hurried along the connecting passage that led to the showroom at the front and deactivated the alarm. Perhaps he was a friend of Ashley's. Perhaps he didn't know she was away. She glanced towards the windows and saw his shadow on the blind. Whatever, she was evidently going to have to deal with him.

Deciding he could wait a few more minutes, Tess turned

5

back into the passageway and entered the small office on the right. This was where Ashley did her paperwork and kept all her records. It was also where she took her breaks and Tess looked longingly at the empty coffee-pot, wishing she had time to fill it.

But Ashley's boss wouldn't be pleased if her tardiness turned a would-be patron away and, after examining her reflection in the small mirror by the door, she pulled a face and went to open the gallery.

The door was glass and, unlike the windows, inset with an iron grille. Taking the precaution of opening all the blinds before she tackled the door, Tess had time to assess her visitor.

He was taller than the average Italian, she saw at once, with dark arresting features. Not handsome, she acknowledged, but she doubted a woman would find that a disadvantage. His features had a dangerous appeal that was purely sexual, a sophisticated savagery that sent a shiver of awareness down her spine.

Oh, yes, she thought, he was exactly the kind of man Ashley would be attracted to, and she guessed his visit to the gallery was of a more personal nature than a commercial one. When she pulled the door wide and secured it in its open position, he arched a faintly mocking brow in recognition of her actions. It made Tess want to close the door again, just to show him how confident she was.

But, instead, she forced a slight smile and said, *'Buongiorno. Posso aiutare?'* in her best schoolgirl Italian.

The man's mouth twitched as if she had said the wrong thing, but he didn't contradict her. Nor did he immediately respond. Pushing his hands into the pockets of his jacket, he swung round and surveyed the contents of the gallery, and Tess wondered if she was wrong about his association with Ashley and that he expected her to give him a guided tour.

Who on earth was he? she wondered, intensely aware of the ambivalence of his gaze. She was sure he wasn't a tourist and it seemed far too early in the day for him to be a serious collector. Besides, the paintings they were exhibiting were hardly a collector's choice.

Realising she was probably completely wrong, she nevertheless suspected he hadn't come here to look at the paintings. Despite his apparent interest, the harsh patrician lines of his profile displayed a contempt for them—or for her. This man would not take rejection easily, she mused, wondering where that thought had come from. But if Ashley was involved, she didn't envy her at all.

Tess hesitated. She wasn't sure whether to leave him to his own devices or ask again if she could help. His elegant charcoal suit—which had to be worth a year's salary to her—made her wish she were wearing something other than an ankle-length cotton skirt and combat boots. The spaghetti straps of her cropped top left her arms bare and she felt horribly exposed suddenly. In her place Ashley would have been wearing heels and a smart outfit. A linen suit, perhaps, with a skirt that barely reached her knees.

Then he turned to face her and she prevented herself from backing up only by a supreme effort of will. Deep-set eyes—golden eyes, she saw incredulously—surveyed her with a studied negligence. She realised he was younger than she'd thought at first and she was again aware of his primitive magnetism. An innate sensual arrogance that left her feeling strangely weak.

'Miss Daniels?' he said smoothly, with barely a trace of an accent. 'It is most—how shall I put it?—enlightening to meet you at last.' He paused. 'I must say, you are not what I expected.' His regard was definitely contemptuous now. 'But still, you will tell me where I might find my son.'

Was that a threat? Tess was taken aback at his tone, but at the same time she realised he had made a mistake. It must be Ashley he wanted, not her. Yet what on earth could Ashley possibly know about his son? She was in England looking after her mother.

'I'm afraid you've made a mistake, *signore*,' she began, only to have him interrupt her.

'No, Miss Daniels, it is you who have made a mistake,' he snapped harshly. 'I know you know where Marco is. My—my *investigatore* saw you getting on a plane together.'

Tess blinked. 'No, you're wrong—'

'Why? Because you are here?' He snapped his long fingers impatiently. 'You bought tickets to Milano but you must have changed planes at Genova. When the plane landed at Malpensa, you and Marco were not on board. *Di conseguenza*, I had no choice but to come here. Be thankful I have found you.'

'But, I'm not—'

'*Prego?*'

'I mean—' Tess knew she sounded crazy '—I'm not Miss Daniels. Well, I am.' Oh, God, if only she could get her words straight. 'But I'm not Miss *Ashley* Daniels. She's my sister.'

The man's eyes conveyed his disbelief. 'Is that the best you can do?'

'It's the truth.' Tess was indignant now. 'My name is Tess. Teresa, actually. But no one calls me that.'

His eyes, those strange predator's eyes, swept over her, rejecting her contention out of hand. 'It's the truth,' she said again, unknowingly defensive. Then, on a wave of inspiration, 'I can prove it. I have my passport with me. Is that good enough for you?'

The man's eyes narrowed. 'Let me see it.'

Tess's eyes widened at the command but there was something about him that made her hurry into the office to collect her bag. The passport was zipped into the side pocket of the backpack and she brought it out triumphantly. But when she turned to go back into the showroom she found he was behind her and with a gesture of defiance she thrust it into his hand.

He was successfully blocking her exit now, she realised, aware of a stirring sense of panic. What did she know about this man, after all? Only that he apparently knew her sister—or rather knew of her—and what he knew seemed hardly flattering.

Or true?

'Look,' she said as he continued to flick through the mostly empty pages of her passport, 'I don't know who you are or what you want but I don't think you have any right to come in here and accuse me—accuse Ashley—of—of—'

'Kidnapping my son?' he suggested scornfully, tossing the passport down onto the desk, and Tess's heart skipped a beat at the ridiculous accusation. '*Attenzione*, Miss Daniels,' he added, sweeping back the thick swathe of dark hair that had invaded his forehead as he studied the pages, 'just because you are not your sister changes nothing. Marco is still missing. He left with your sister. Therefore, you must have some idea where they are.'

'No!' Tess hardly knew what she was saying. 'I mean—I do know where Ashley is. She's at her mother's house in England. Her mother is ill. Ashley is looking after her.'

His expression didn't alter. 'And that is why you are here taking her place?'

'Yes. I'm a schoolteacher. I was on holiday. That's how I was able to help her out.'

'You are lying, Miss Daniels. Why are you not caring for your mother? I have just read in your passport that you live in England. So tell me why you are not taking care of your mother in your sister's place?'

'She's not *my* mother,' Tess exclaimed hotly. 'My father married again after my mother died.' She took a deep breath. 'Now, I think that answers your question. I'm sorry your son is missing but it's nothing to do with us.'

'You are wrong.' He didn't accept her explanation but at least he stepped back into the passageway to give her some room. When Tess escaped into the comparative safety of the showroom, he followed her. 'Whatever you say, Miss Daniels, your sister is not caring for her sick mother,' he insisted. 'She and Marco are still in Italy. He does not have his passport with him, *capisce*?'

Tess pressed nervous hands to her bare midriff, feeling the quivering beat of her heart palpating between her ribs. 'You said—she'd kidnapped him,' she reminded him tensely. 'That's a ridiculous accusation. If—and it's a big if—Ashley and your son are together, then surely that's their affair, not yours?'

'*Non credo*. I do not think so.' He was contemptuous. 'My son is sixteen years of age, Miss Daniels. He belongs in school, with young people of his own age, not chasing around the country after your sister.'

Tess swallowed convulsively. Sixteen! She couldn't believe it. Ashley wouldn't—couldn't—be involved with a boy of sixteen! The whole idea was laughable. Involved with *him*, perhaps. That Tess could believe. But not with his teenage son.

Besides, she told herself again, clinging to what she knew and not what he suspected, Ashley was in England. Dammit, she'd spoken to her just a couple of nights ago. That was why Tess was spending part of her Easter break filling in for her. Ashley couldn't leave the gallery unattended and she'd promised it would only be for a few days.

'If you've not met my sister, how can you be sure that she's involved?' she asked unwillingly, realising she couldn't dismiss his claim out of hand. Ashley might not have been in England when she'd phoned her. She could have used her mobile. How could she be sure?

The man gave her an impatient look now. 'I may have met her once, but that was some months ago and I have met many people since then. In any case, the person who has been watching her would not make a mistake. I have been out of the country, regrettably, but my assistant contacted your sister just a week ago. She swore then that she would speak to Marco, that she would tell him there was no future in their—association. She is what? Twenty-four? Twenty-five? Much too old for a boy of sixteen.'

Tess pressed her lips together. 'She's twenty-eight, actually,' she said, as if that made any difference, and watched his scowl deepen as he absorbed her words. She didn't know what to say; she hardly knew what to think. But if it was true, she agreed with him. Could Ashley have told her an outright lie?

She could, she reflected ruefully. And she had to admit that when Ashley had asked her to help her out while she took care of her mother, it had seemed a little out of character. Ashley's mother, Andrea, had never been a particularly strong woman and since their father had died of a heart attack just over a year ago, she'd suffered from a series of minor complaints. Tess had suspected that that was why Ashley had taken this job in Italy. Looking after a fretful parent who was halfway to being a hypochondriac had never seemed her style.

All the same, this situation was no less incredible. Surely even Ashley would draw the line at getting involved with a boy of sixteen? There was only one way to find out and that was to ring Ashley's mother. But Tess was loath to do it. If Ashley was there, it would look as if she didn't trust her.

'I don't know what to say,' she murmured now, her fingers threading anxiously through the wisps of pale blonde hair at her nape. She'd had her hair cut before she came away and she wasn't totally convinced the gamine style suited her. She'd hoped it would give her some maturity, but she had the feeling it hadn't succeeded. He was looking at her as if she were no older than one of her own pupils. Oh, Lord, what was she going to do?

'You could tell me where they are,' the man declared tersely. 'I realise you must feel some loyalty towards your sister, but you must also see that this situation cannot be allowed to continue.'

'I don't know where they are,' Tess insisted. 'Honestly, I don't.' And then, realising what she'd said, she added hastily, 'As far as I know, Ashley's in England, as I said.'

'*Bene,* then you can ring her,' he said, voicing the thought

Tess had had a few minutes before. 'If she is with her mother, I will offer you my sincerest apologies for troubling you.'

'And if she's not?'

Tess looked up at him, unable to disguise her apprehension, and for a moment she thought he was going to relent. But then, with a tightening of his lips, he corrected her. 'You are confident she will be there,' he said, and she had the fanciful thought that this man would take no prisoners. She just hoped Ashley had taken that into consideration before she'd taken off with his son.

If she'd taken off with his son, she amended sharply. She only had his word for that. And that of his *investigatore*—his investigator, she assumed. But she was becoming far too willing to accept what this man said as if it was the truth.

'If—if she is there, who shall I say is asking for her?' she inquired abruptly, realising she had been staring at him for far too long. He probably thought she was a flake in her long skirt and combat boots, she reflected ruefully. After all this, it wouldn't do for him to think that Ashley's sister might be interested in him.

He hesitated a moment, evidently considering her question. Then, he said briefly, 'Just tell her it is Castelli. The name will mean something to her, I am sure.'

Tess guessed it would, though what she didn't dare to speculate. Oh, please, she begged, let Ashley be staying with her mother. Apart from anything else, Tess was going to look such a gullible fool if she wasn't.

'All right,' she declared briskly. 'I'll ring her. If you'd like to give me a number where I can reach you, I'll let you know what she says.'

'If she says anything,' murmured Castelli wryly, and then his dark brows drew together. 'But perhaps you would ring her now, Miss Daniels? I will wait while you make the call.'

Tess caught her breath. He was certainly determined to have his way. But she'd been chivvied long enough. 'I can't ring her now,' she said, not allowing him to intimidate her.

'I'll ring her later. And now, if you'll excuse me, I've got work to do.'

His scepticism was evident. 'You have?' He glanced round the gallery. 'You are not exactly overrun with customers, Miss Daniels.'

Tess stiffened her spine. 'Look, I've said I'll ring Ashley and I will. Isn't that enough for you?' The underlying words were almost audible. *But not until you have gone!*

His faint smile was sardonic. 'You are afraid to make the call, Miss Daniels,' he said impatiently. 'Be careful, or I shall begin to think you have been lying to me all along.'

Tess's anger was hot and unexpected. 'Oh, please,' she exclaimed fiercely. 'I don't have to listen to this. It's not my fault if your son's been foolish enough to get involved with an older woman. You're his father. Don't you have some responsibility here?'

For a moment, his stillness terrified her. He was like a predator, she thought unsteadily, and she waited in a panic for him to spring. But suddenly his lips twitched into a smile that was blatantly sensual. A look, almost of admiration, crossed his dark face and he appraised her small indignant figure with a rueful gaze.

'*Dio mio,*' he said, and her heart quickened instinctively. 'The little cat has claws.'

His analogy was startling. It was so close to what she had been thinking about him. Though he was no domesticated feline, she acknowledged urgently. Those strange tawny eyes belonged to a different beast entirely.

And, despite her determination not to let him have his way, she found herself stammering an apology. 'I'm—I'm sorry,' she said. 'I shouldn't have spoken as I did. It—it's nothing to do with me.'

'*No, mi scusi, signorina,*' he said. 'You are right. This is not your problem. Regrettably, my son has always been a little—what is it you say?—headstrong? I should not have allowed my anger with him to spill over onto you.'

Tess quivered. His eyes were softer now, gentler, a mesmerising deepening of colour that turned them almost opaque. They were locked on hers and the breath seemed to leave her body. Oh, God, she shivered, the impact on her senses leaving her feeling absurdly vulnerable. What was wrong with her? She was behaving as if a man had never looked at her before.

'It doesn't matter,' she managed at last, but he wouldn't let it go.

'It does matter,' he said. 'I am an unfeeling moron, and I should not have called your honesty into question. If you will give me your sister's number, I will make the call myself.'

Tess stifled a groan. Dear Lord, just as she was beginning to think the worst was over, he sprang this on her. Having reduced her to mush with his eyes, he was now moving in for the kill. He hadn't given up. He'd only changed his tactics. And she couldn't be absolutely sure that this hadn't been his intention all along.

She moved her head in a helpless gesture. How could she give him the number? How could she allow him to speak to Ashley's mother if Ashley wasn't there? Andrea would have a fit if he told her that her daughter was missing. And if he added that he suspected she was with his sixteen-year-old son, heaven knew how Ashley's mother would react.

Concentrating her gaze on the pearl-grey silk knot of his tie, Tess strove for a reason not to give the number to him. But it was hard enough to find excuses for her reaction to a stranger without the added burden of her own guilt. 'I—don't think that would be a very good idea,' she said, wishing desperately that someone else would come into the gallery. But no one did, and she continued unevenly, 'Ashley's mother isn't well. I wouldn't want to upset her.'

Castelli heaved a sigh. '*Signorina*—'

'Please: call me Tess.'

He expelled a breath. 'Tess, then,' he agreed, though she hardly recognised her name on his tongue. His faint accent gave it a foreign sibilance that was strange and melodic.

'Why would my call upset her? I have no intention of intimidating anyone.'

But he did, thought Tess grimly, almost without his being
aware of it. It was in his genes, an aristocratic arrogance
that was dominant in his blood. Who was he? she wondered
again. What was his background? And what did his wife
think of the situation? Was she as opposed to the liaison as
he was?

Of course she must be, Tess told herself severely, averting
eyes that had strayed almost irresistibly back to his face.
But if Marco was like his father, she could understand
Ashley's attraction. If she had been attracted to his son, she
amended. She must not jump to conclusions here.

'I—Mrs Daniels doesn't know you,' she said firmly, answering his question. 'And—and if by chance Ashley is out
and she answers the phone, she's bound to be concerned.'

'Why?' Once again those disturbing eyes invaded her
space. 'Come, Tess, why not be honest? You are afraid that
your sister is not at her mother's house. Am I not correct?'

Tess's defensive gaze betrayed her. 'All right,' she said
unwillingly. 'I admit, there is a possibility—a small possibility—that Ashley isn't in England, after all. But—' she
put up a hand when he would have interrupted her and continued '—that doesn't mean she's with—with Marco. With
your son.' The boy's name came far too easily. 'She might
just have decided she needed a break and, as it's the Easter
holidays, I was available.'

'You do not believe that,' he told her softly, running a
questing hand down the silken length of his tie. The gesture
was unconsciously sensual, though she doubted he was
aware of it. Sensuality was part of his persona. Like his lean,
intriguing face and the powerful body beneath his sleek
Armani suit. 'I also think you are far too understanding. I
hope your sister realises what a loyal little friend she has in
you.'

It was the 'little' that did it. Tess had spent her life in-
sisting that people not judge her by her size. 'All right,' she

said again, anger giving her a confidence she hadn't been able to summon earlier. 'I'll phone her. Now. But if she is there—'

'I will find some suitable means of recompense,' he finished softly. 'And if your sister is like you, then I can understand why Marco found her so—appealing.'

'Don't patronise me!' Tess was incensed by his condescension. 'As it happens, Ashley's nothing like me. She's tall and more—more—' How could she say curvaceous to him? 'Um—she's dark and I'm fair.'

'So…' His tone was almost indulgent now. 'Once again, I have offended you, *cara*. Forgive me. I suppose, being the younger sister—'

'I'm not the younger sister,' Tess broke in hotly, wondering why she'd ever thought that cutting her hair would make a difference. 'I told you, my father married again after my mother died.'

'*Non posso crederci!* I can't believe it.' He shook his head. 'But you told me your sister was twenty-eight, *no*?'

'And I'm thirty-two,' said Tess shortly, struggling to hold on to her patience. She paused, and then in a more civil tone she added, 'Don't bother to tell me I don't look it. I've spent the last ten years trying to convince people that I'm older than the kids I teach.'

Castelli's mouth tilted at the corners and she was struck anew by his disturbing appeal. 'Most women would envy you, Tess. My own mother spends a small fortune on retaining her youth.'

'But I am not most women,' she retorted, realising she was only putting off the inevitable. 'And now, I suppose, I'd better make that call.'

CHAPTER TWO

RAFE DI CASTELLI paced tensely about the gallery. All his instincts were urging him to join her in the small office, to be present while she made the call. To make sure she actually called her sister, he conceded tersely. Despite her apparent innocence, he had no reason to trust Tess Daniels any more than her sister.

But courtesy—and an underlying belief that she wouldn't lie to him—kept him out of earshot. He didn't want to know how she phrased her question; he didn't want to hear her distress if he was right. And he was right, he told himself grimly. Verdicci had been adamant. Two people had got aboard the plane to Milano, and one of them had been his son.

It seemed to take for ever. He was fairly sure her Italian wasn't fluent and it might have been easier if he had placed the call for her. But any suggestion of involvement on his part would have seemed like interference. Besides, impatient as he was, he was prepared to give her the time to marshal her thoughts.

She emerged from the office a few moments later and he saw at once that she was upset. Her hair was rumpled, as if she'd been running agitated fingers through it as she spoke, and her winter-pale cheeks were bright with colour.

She looked delectable, he thought ruefully, despising the impulse that would put such a thought in his mind at this time. Was this how she looked when she left her bed? he wondered. All pale tangled hair and face flushed from sleep?

It was a curiously disturbing picture, and one that he chose to ignore. Engaging though she was, she could mean nothing to him. He was amused by her naïvety, but that was all.

'She's not there,' she burst out abruptly as he paused, expectantly, looking at her. 'Andrea—that's Ashley's mother—she hasn't seen her.'

Rafe felt a mixture of resignation and relief. Resignation that his information had been correct, and relief that there was not some unknown woman involved.

'You knew that, of course,' she went on, regarding him half resentfully. Green eyes, fringed by surprisingly dark lashes, surveyed him without liking. 'So—you were right and I was wrong. What do we do now?'

'We?' Her use of the personal pronoun caused an automatic arching of his brows and she had the grace to look embarrassed at her presumption.

'I mean, I—that is, me,' she fumbled. 'What am I going to do now? I can't stay here indefinitely. I'm due back at school in ten days' time.'

'As is Marco,' he observed drily, feeling a little of her frustration himself. 'May I ask, what did your sister tell you when she handed the keys of the gallery to you? Did she give you any idea when she would return?'

Tess sighed. 'I haven't seen Ashley,' she muttered, lifting both hands to cup her neck, and his eyes were unwillingly drawn to the widening gap of skin at her midriff. Such soft skin it looked, creamy and flawless. Such a contrast to the ugly boots she wore on her feet.

Dragging his thoughts out of the gutter, Rafe tried to absorb what she was saying. 'You have not seen her,' he echoed blankly. 'I do not understand.'

'Ashley phoned me,' she explained. 'She said her mother was ill and was there any chance that I could come here and look after the gallery for a few days while she went to England. She said she wanted to leave immediately. That she was worried about her mother and she'd leave the keys with the caretaker of her apartment.'

'So you crossed in transit?'

'In a manner of speaking. But Ashley's mother and I live in different parts of the country.'

'Ah.' He nodded. 'So your sister had every reason to believe that she would not be found out in her deception.'

'I suppose so.' Clearly she didn't want to admit it, but Rafe could see the acknowledgement in her face. She shook her head. 'I can't believe she'd think she'd get away with it. I could have phoned Andrea. I could have found out she wasn't ill for myself.'

'But you did not?'

'No.' Tess shrugged her slim shoulders and her hands dropped to her sides. 'Ashley knows I was unlikely to do that, in any case. Andrea and I have never been particularly close.'

'Yet you must have been very young when your mother died,' he probed, and then could have kicked himself for his insensitivity. But it was too late now and he was forced to explain himself. 'I assumed this woman—your father's second wife—would have cared for you, too.'

Tess shook her head. 'Andrea has always been a—a delicate woman,' she said. 'Having two young children to look after would have been too much for her. I went to live with my mother's sister. She'd never married and she was a teacher, too.'

Poor Tess. Rafe made no comment, but it sounded to him as if Andrea Daniels was as unfeeling and as selfish as her daughter. 'It seems we have both been deceived,' he said, softening his tone deliberately. 'It is a pity your sister does not carry a mobile. Marco's is switched off.'

'But she does,' exclaimed Tess excitedly, animation giving her porcelain-pale features a startling allure. Her smile appeared and Rafe had to warn himself of the dangers of responding to her femininity. 'Why didn't I think of it before? She gave me the number when she moved to Porto San Michele.'

Rafe expelled a harsh breath. 'You have the number with you?'

'Of course.' She swung about and headed back into the office where she'd left her bag. She emerged a few seconds later, clutching a scrap of paper. 'Here it is. Do you want to ring her, or shall I?'

Rafe realised suddenly that, almost without his volition, they had become co-conspirators. She was now as anxious to know where her sister had gone as he was. But once again he reminded himself not to get involved with her, however innocently. She was still his enemy's sister. In any conflict of wills, she would choose Ashley every time.

'If you wish that I should make the call, then I will,' he told her politely, but he could hear the formal stiffness in his tone. 'Even so, perhaps it would be wiser for you to phone her. If she hears my voice...'

'Oh. Oh, yes.'

He didn't elaborate but Tess understood at once what he was saying. The animation died out of her face and she averted her eyes. It was as if she'd just remembered that she owed him no favours either. That however justified he felt, she had only his word that Ashley was to blame for his son's disappearance.

With an offhand little gesture, she returned to the office, only to emerge again a few minutes later, her expression revealing she had had no luck. 'Ashley's phone is switched off, too,' she said, and Rafe could see she was losing faith in her sister. She heaved a sigh. 'It looks as if you were right all along. What are you going to do now?'

Rafe wished he had an answer. There was hardly any point in saying what he'd like to do. 'Continue searching, *presumo*,' he replied at last, choosing the least aggressive option. 'There are many holiday resorts between here and Genova. It is possible that your sister hired an automobile at the airport. They could be anywhere. It will not be an easy task.'

'Mmm.' Tess was thoughtful. A pink tongue circled her lower lip and Rafe realised she didn't know how provocative that was. 'Will you let me know if you find them?' she asked 'I mean—find Ashley.' Becoming colour scored her cheeks. 'You know what I mean.'

Rafe knew what she meant all right. What he didn't know at that moment was whether he wanted to see her again. She was far too young for him, far too vulnerable. Despite her being the older, he'd stake his life that Ashley was far more worldly than she was.

The notion annoyed him however. What in the name of all the saints was he thinking? She wasn't asking to see him again. She was asking if he'd keep her informed about her sister. *Va bene*, he could get his assistant to do that with a phone call. Providing he found out where her sister had gone…

'*Sì*,' he said abruptly, buttoning his jacket in an unconsciously defensive gesture and heading for the door. He turned in the doorway, however, to bid her farewell and was surprised by a strangely disappointed look on her face. With her slim hands clasped at her waist, she looked lost and lonely, and before he could stop himself he added, 'Perhaps you could do the same?'

Her green eyes widened. 'I don't know where to reach you,' she said, as he'd known she would. *Maledizione*, he hadn't intended to give her his phone number. How easily he'd fallen into the trap.

He would have to give her his card, he decided, reaching into his jacket pocket. That way Giulio could handle it and he needn't be involved. To give her his mobile number would have been kinder, obviously, but why should he put himself out for the sister of the woman who had seduced his son?

He took a few paces back into the gallery and handed the card to her. Her fingers brushed his knuckles as she took it and he couldn't deny the sudden frisson of desire that seared his flesh. He wanted her, he thought incredulously. Combat boots and all, she attracted him. Or maybe he was feeling his age and seducing her would give him some compensation for what her sister had done to Marco. What other reason could he have for the feelings she inspired?

Whatever, he dismissed the idea impatiently. He was obviously having some kind of midlife crisis because girls like Tess had never appealed to him before. He liked his women young—well, reasonably so, but far more sophisticated. They wore designer dresses and heels, and they'd never dream of going out without make-up on their faces.

Vigneto di Castelli, his card read, and he watched Tess's expression as she looked at it. 'You have a vineyard,' she murmured. 'How exciting! I've never met anyone who actually owned a vineyard before.'

Nor had her sister, thought Rafe drily. He was too cynical to believe that Marco's background hadn't figured in Ashley's plans. He still had no idea what her ultimate intentions were, of course, but he suspected that a pay-off would be part of it. He'd encountered the ploy before with his daughter. But fortunately Maria had been eighteen, not sixteen at the time.

'It is a small operation, *signorina*,' he said now deprecatingly. 'Many families in Italy have taken to growing grapes with the increase in wine drinking in recent years.'

'All the same…' Her lips curved beguilingly, and Rafe felt the familiar pull of awareness inside him. Time to go, he thought grimly, before he invited her to visit the villa. He could just imagine his mother's horror if he returned home with someone like Tess in tow.

'*Ci vediamo, signorina,*' he said politely as he retraced his steps to the door but she wouldn't let him have the last word.

'My name's Tess,' she reminded him, following him out onto the esplanade and watching as he strode away towards his car.

And, although he didn't answer her, he knew that was how he would think of her. Somehow the name suited her personality. It was as capricious and feminine as she was.

* * *

As he'd half expected, his mother was waiting for him when he returned to the Villa Castelli.

A tall, elegant woman in her mid-sixties, she'd moved back into the villa six years ago when he'd divorced his wife. Rafe's father had died almost twenty years before and he was sure that looking after Maria and Marco had given the old lady a new lease of life. Of course, she'd never forgiven him for divorcing Gina. In the Castelli family marriages were made to last and her strict religious beliefs rebelled against such secular freedom. Nevertheless, she had proved a tower of strength on many occasions and it was only recently that she had decided that the time had come to move back into the small farmhouse she'd occupied on the estate since Raphael's father's death.

Rafe knew her decision had been partly influenced by his son's behaviour. Although Maria had had her own period of rebellion, she had been fairly easy to control in comparison to her brother. Marco was self-willed and headstrong— much as he had been at the same age, Rafe acknowledged honestly—but without the sense of responsibility his father had instilled in him.

'You've seen her?'

His mother's first words reminded Rafe that, as far as Lucia di Castelli was concerned, Ashley Daniels was still running the Medici Gallery. His main reason for visiting the gallery had been to find out if Ashley knew where Marco was hiding. Instead of which he'd met her sister and discovered he was not too old to make a fool of himself, too.

'She's not at the gallery,' he said with contrived carelessness, strolling onto the loggia where his mother was waiting enjoying a mid-morning *cappuccino*. It was very warm on the loggia and Rafe loosened his tie and pulled it a couple of inches away from his collar before approaching a glass-topped table and helping himself to one of the thin, honey-soaked *biscotti* Lucia loved. 'Verdicci appears to have been correct. They have gone away together.' He glanced round as a uniformed maid came to ask if there was anything he required. 'Just coffee, Sophia,' he replied pleasantly. 'Black.' Then to his mother. 'Her sister is looking after the gallery while she's away.'

'Her sister?'

His mother was sceptical, and Rafe guessed she'd jumped to the same conclusion he had. 'Her sister,' he confirmed, flinging himself into a cane-backed chair and staring broodingly out across the gardens below the terrace. 'Believe me, she is nothing like this woman Marco has got himself involved with.'

'How do you know this?' Lucia's dark eyes narrowed. 'I thought you said you wouldn't recognise the woman if you saw her.'

'I wouldn't.' Rafe realised he had been far too definite. 'But Tess is a schoolteacher. And, believe me, she's as much in the dark as we are. Ashley had given her some story about going home to care for her sick mother.'

'*Tess!*' Lucia scoffed. 'What kind of a name is that?'

'It's Teresa,' replied Rafe evenly, thanking the maid who had delivered his coffee. He turned back to his mother in some irritation. 'We won't get anywhere by picking fault with one of the few people who might be able to help us.'

'How can this woman help us? You said yourself she doesn't know where her sister is.'

'Ashley may get in touch with her. If she wants Teresa to go on believing the story she's given her, she may feel the need to embellish it in some way.'

Lucia's mouth drew into a thin line. 'It sounds to me as if this—this sister of the Daniels woman has made quite an impression on you, Raphael,' she declared tersely. 'Why do you believe her? What proof do you have that she's telling you the truth?'

None at all! 'Believe me, she was as shocked as we were,' he responded stiffly. 'You can't blame her for what her sister's done.'

'And has she contacted her mother?' Lucia was scathing.

'Forgive me, I know I'm old-fashioned, but don't English girls keep in touch with their own parents these days?'

'Of course they do,' retorted Rafe testily. 'But Ashley's mother isn't her mother. Their father married twice. Teresa is the older sister.'

'Che sorpresa!' What a surprise! Lucia was sardonic. 'People get married and divorced at the drop of a hat these days.' She crossed herself before continuing. 'Thank Jesu for the Holy Catholic church. At least most good Catholics take their vows seriously.'

Rafe knew that was directed at him but he chose not to rise to it. It wasn't worth it. He contented himself with saying drily, 'I understand Teresa's mother is dead.' Then, refusing to feel defensive, added, 'In any case, as you'll have guessed, Ashley wasn't at her mother's home. It seems she has told her sister a pack of lies.'

Lucia shook her head. 'It sounds very suspicious to me.'

Rafe controlled his temper with an effort. 'Well, I cannot help that,' he said grimly.

'But you must admit it is strange that this woman—this Teresa—doesn't know where her sister is.' She arched an aristocratic eyebrow. 'Why on earth would she want to keep her whereabouts a secret from her?'

'Because she knew her sister wouldn't approve any more than we do?' suggested Rafe tightly. 'I don't know, Mama. But I believe her and I think you should do the same.'

Lucia sniffed and Rafe thought how ridiculous this was, having to explain himself to his mother. Sometimes she behaved as if he were no older than Marco. He supposed it came of giving her free rein with the household after Gina walked out.

'So what happens now?' she inquired at last when it became obvious that Rafe was going to say no more. 'Do I take it that unless the woman gets in touch with her sister, the information Verdicci gave you is our only lead?'

'I will also speak to Maria,' said Rafe. 'She and Marco share most things and she may know where he's gone. It's a long shot and for the present we only know they disembarked in Genova. I suspect the Daniels woman guessed we might check the airlines and buying tickets to Milano was meant to throw us off the scent.'

'And knowing they might be in Genova helps us how?'

'Well, obviously she didn't know we were watching her. She has no reason to believe that we might question whether they completed their journey. Ergo, she will expect us to make inquiries in Milano. Inquiries which, as we now know, would have gained us nothing.'

'Very well.' Lucia accepted his reasoning. 'But Genova is a big city. How do you propose to find them there?'

'I'm hoping Ashley will have hired an automobile,' replied Rafe, finishing his coffee and getting to his feet again. He paced somewhat restlessly across the terrazzo tiles, staring out at the distant vineyard, hazy in the morning sunshine. 'Verdicci is checking the rental agencies at the airport. If she has used her own name, we will find them, never fear.'

'And if she hasn't?'

'Car rental agencies need identification. If my guess is correct, she will have used her passport to confirm her identity. Either that or her work permit. In each case, she will have had to use her own name. She may even have had to give an address—a local address, I mean. Somewhere she plans to stay. Where *they* plan to stay.'

Lucia's lips crumpled. 'Oh, this is so terrible! Every time I close my eyes, all I can see is Marco and that woman, together. It's—appalling! Disgusting!'

'Don't exaggerate, Mama.' Rafe could see she was building up to another hysterical outburst. His lips twisted. 'For all I know, Marco may be more experienced than we thought. He must have something to have attracted the interest of a woman of her age.'

'Don't be offensive!' Lucia gazed at him with horrified eyes. 'How can you even say such things? Marco is just a child—'

'He's nearly seventeen, Mama.' Rafe was impatient now. 'He's not a child. He's a young man.' He paused. 'With a young man's needs and—desires.'

Lucia's spine stiffened and she pushed herself rigidly to her feet. 'Very well,' she said coldly. 'I can see you are not prepared to discuss this sensibly so I might as well go. I should have expected this of you, of course. You've never taken a strong enough hand with that boy and now we're all suffering the consequences.'

Rafe blew out a breath. 'You're not suffering anything, Mama. Except perhaps from a little jealousy. I know you've always thought the sun shone out of Marco's—well, you've always favoured him over Maria. Perhaps you ought to wonder if you are in any way responsible for his apparent rebellion against parental authority.'

Lucia's jaw dropped. 'You can't blame me?'

'I'm not blaming anyone,' retorted Rafe wearily. 'You are. All I'm doing is defending myself.'

'As you did when Gina decided she'd had enough of your indifference?' declared his mother tersely, making for the door. 'You've always neglected your family, Raphael. First your wife and now your son. With you, your work must always come first.'

'Gina slept with my estate manager,' said Rafe through his teeth, but Lucia was not deterred.

'She was lonely, Raphael. She needed love and you didn't give it to her. What did you expect?'

Trust? Loyalty? Rafe didn't attempt to dispute her words, however. This was an old argument and one he had no intention of rekindling. Gina hadn't wanted love, she'd wanted sex. Her affair with Guido Marchetta might have been the reason he'd divorced her, but it hadn't been the first. He had never told his mother that and now was not the time to do so.

'Look,' he said, his tone neutral. 'Let's not get into blaming ourselves. Marco's somewhere out there and I'm going to find him.'

Lucia shrugged. 'If you can,' she said scornfully, determined to have the last word, and Rafe let her enjoy her small victory.

CHAPTER THREE

As Tess had half expected, Ashley's mother rang the gallery just after the man, Castelli, had left.

Tess didn't blame her. She wouldn't have been satisfied with the terse explanation she had given her. But once Tess had ascertained that Ashley wasn't there, all she'd wanted to do was get off the phone. It had been bad enough having to relay the news to Castelli. Discussing Ashley's whereabouts with her mother while he'd listened in just hadn't been possible.

Even so, when the phone pealed in the small office she paused a moment to pray that it might be her sister instead. The gallery was still empty and she had no excuse for not answering it. And it could be anyone, she reminded herself, not looking forward to explaining the situation to Andrea.

'Teresa?' Clearly Ashley's mother had no difficulty in distinguishing between their voices. 'What's going on? What are you doing at the gallery? Where's Ashley?'

Tess sighed. When she'd spoken to Andrea earlier, she hadn't mentioned the gallery. But it was only natural that Andrea would ring here when she got no reply from Tess's flat. And this was where her daughter was supposed to be, after all.

'Um—she's taking a holiday,' Tess managed at last, deciding that the best liars were those who stuck most closely to the truth. 'It's good to hear from you, Andrea. How are you?'

'Never mind how I am, Teresa.' There was no affection in the older woman's voice. 'Five minutes ago you rang here asking to speak to Ashley. You must have known how

29

upsetting that would be for me. As far as I knew, she was still in Porto San Michele.'

'You've heard from her?'

Tess couldn't keep the excitement out of her voice and her stepmother detected it. 'Of course, I've heard from her,' she said shortly. And then, more suspiciously, 'Why shouldn't I? She still cares about me, you know.'

'Well, of course she does—'

'Just because you encouraged her to leave home and live alone, as you do, doesn't mean Ashley doesn't have a conscience,' continued Andrea preposterously. 'I know you've always been jealous of our relationship, Teresa, but if this is some ploy to try and get me to think badly of—'

'It's not.'

Tess couldn't even begin to unravel what Andrea was talking about. She hadn't encouraged Ashley to leave home and work in Italy. She had certainly never been jealous of her relationship with her mother. Envious, perhaps, because her own mother wasn't there to share her hopes and fears; her development. But Aunt Kate had been a wonderful substitute. And what she'd lacked in experience, she'd more than made up for in love.

'Then why ring me?' demanded Andrea accusingly. 'Worrying me unnecessarily, making me wonder if something terrible had happened to her.'

'It's not like that.'

'Then what is it like? You ask me if I've heard from her as if she's gone missing. Don't you have her mobile phone number? Why don't you ring her on that?'

Tess hesitated. 'Her phone's not working,' she admitted. 'And—well, I just wondered if Ashley had gone to England after all. As you'll have guessed, I'm looking after the gallery while she's away.' She paused, seeking inspiration, and then added unwillingly, 'I—I had a customer of hers asking about—a painting.' *Liar!* 'I—I just thought it was worth seeing if she was staying with you.'

Andrea snorted disbelievingly, and Tess felt a growing

sense of injustice at the impossible position Ashley had put her in. Not only had she left her to deal with her boyfriend's irate father, but she must have known Tess might ring her mother when she believed that that was where Ashley was.

All the same, it wasn't in Tess's nature to upset anyone unnecessarily, and, taking a deep breath, she said, 'I'm sure she'll be in touch with me again in a few days.' She'll have to, Tess added to herself. Ashley knew she was due back at school in ten days as well. 'But—um—if you hear from her in the meantime, could you ask her to ring me? The—er— the customer I was telling you about, he is pretty eager to speak to Ashley himself.'

Andrea was silent for so long that Tess began to hope that she'd pacified the woman. But just as she was about to excuse herself on the pretext that someone had come into the gallery Ashley's mother spoke again.

'And you have absolutely no idea where Ashley is?' she asked again urgently, a worrying tremor in her voice. 'If you do know anything, Teresa, I demand that you tell me. Do you think I should come out there? If Ashley's missing, the police ought to be informed.'

'Ashley's not missing.' Tess hurried to reassure her, cursing her sister anew for getting her into this mess. 'Honestly, Andrea, there's no need for you to concern yourself. Ashley's taken a break, that's all. She's probably turned off her phone so she isn't bothered with nuisance calls.'

'I hope you're not suggesting that if I ring my daughter she'd regard it as a nuisance call!' exclaimed Andrea at once, but at least the disturbing tremor had left her voice.

'Of course not,' protested Tess, determining to find out exactly what Ashley had been telling her mother about their relationship. Andrea hadn't always treated her kindly, but she hadn't regarded Tess as an enemy before.

'Oh, well…' There was resignation in the woman's voice now. 'I suppose I have to take your word for it. But, re-member, I expect you to keep me informed if there are any developments. And if you hear from Ashley, you can tell her that I expect her to ring me at once.'

'Okay.'

Somehow, Tess found the right words to end the conversation, and with a feeling of immense relief she put the handset down. But her sense of indignation didn't end when she severed the connection. She was beginning to feel distinctly put upon and she wished she'd never agreed to come here in the first place.

An image of Castelli flashed before her eyes, but she refused to acknowledge it. She had no intention of allowing her interview with the Italian to influence her mood. Besides which, he was just someone else who regarded her as unworthy of his respect.

She scowled. This was not the way Ashley had sold this trip to her. Her sister had asked her to babysit the gallery, true, but she'd also sweetened the request with promises of long sunny days and evenings spent exploring the bars and *ristorantes* of the popular resort. Not that Tess cared much for bars, but the idea of eating in real Italian restaurants had been appealing. And, like anyone else who held down a job, she'd looked forward to spending some time on the beach.

Now it was all spoilt. After spending the first couple of evenings tidying Ashley's apartment and making sense of her bookkeeping, she was confronted by this situation. It was typical of Ashley, she thought flatly. Typical of her sister to trample over everyone's feelings if it made her happy. And there was no doubt that Ashley had known how Tess would have reacted if she'd told her what she'd intended. That was why she'd made sure she'd been long gone before Tess had arrived.

It was so frustrating; so disappointing. She should have guessed there was more to it than Ashley had told her. She should have rung Andrea before she'd left England. It was her own fault for not expressing any interest in her stepmother's health. But for now she was helpless. Until Ashley chose to contact her, there was nothing she could do.

She had planned on treating herself to an evening meal at the local *pizzeria* before returning to the apartment, but she changed her mind. After spending an uneasy day jumping every time someone came into the gallery, she was in no mood for company. She would buy herself some salad greens, she thought, toss them in a lemon vinaigrette, and grate some parmesan for flavour.

She was about to lock up when a man appeared in the doorway. He had his back to the light and for a ridiculous moment she thought Castelli had come back. Her heart skipped a beat and hot colour surged into her throat. But then the man moved and she realised her mistake.

It was Silvio Palmieri, she saw at once, the young man who ran the sports shop next door. Though perhaps calling the establishment he managed a sports shop was understating the obvious, Tess mused. With its windows full of endorsements from famous sports personalities and the exclusive designer gear it sold, it was definitely not just a sports shop.

Still, she acknowledged she had been foolish to mistake the younger man for Castelli. Silvio was dark, it was true, but that was where the resemblance ended. He didn't move with the instinctive grace of a predator or regard her with tawny-eyed suspicion. Silvio was just a rather pleasant man who had taken it upon himself to look out for her.

'*Ciao,*' he said. Then he noticed her expression. '*Mi scusi*, I startle you, *no*?'

'Oh—I was miles away,' murmured Tess, gathering her composure. 'You surprised me, that's all.'

Silvio frowned. 'You have not had bad news?' he asked, with surprising perception. 'Ashley's mama—she has not had a relapse, *spero*?'

'Not as far as I know,' said Tess drily, not at all sure how Andrea must be feeling at this moment. 'Um—have you had a good day?'

Silvio shrugged. 'What do you say? So-so? *Sì*, it has been a so-so day. How about you?'

Tess felt an almost irresistible urge to laugh, but she doubted Silvio would appreciate her hysterics. She couldn't involve him in her problems. Ashley wouldn't like it and Castelli definitely wouldn't approve.

'It's been—interesting,' she said, moving to drop the blinds on the windows. 'But I'm not sorry it's over.' And that was the truth.

'I saw Raphael di Castelli come into the gallery earlier,' Silvio ventured, his brows raised in inquiry, and Tess wondered if she was being absurdly suspicious in thinking that that was the real reason he had come. 'He is quite a well-known person in San Michele. In the season, many people work at the villa. Picking the grapes, *capisce*?'

Tess stared at him. 'You know him?' she asked, absorbing the fact that his name was *Raphael di* Castelli. She moistened her lips. 'Does he have a large vineyard, then?'

'I think so.' Silvio was regarding her curiously now. 'And, no, I do not know him. Well, not personally, you understand?'

Tess hesitated. Ashley's interest in Marco was beginning to make sense. 'And Ashley?' she asked, trying to sound casual. 'I believe she knows his son?'

'Ah, Marco.' Silvio nodded. '*Sì*. Marco is—how do you say?—the artist, *no*?'

'Marco's a painter?'

'He would like to be.' Silvio spread a hand towards the paintings lining the walls of the gallery. 'He would like the exhibition, I think.'

Tess caught her breath. Castelli hadn't mentioned that his son wanted to be a painter. But perhaps it explained how Ashley had come to know Marco, however.

Now she looked around. 'Are any of these his paintings?' she asked cautiously and Silvio laughed.

'*A mala pena.*' Hardly. 'But he is ambitious, *no*?'

'I see.' Tess nodded. 'Does his father approve?'

'I think not,' said Silvio, sobering. 'Di Castellis do not

waste their time with such pursuits. Besides, Marco is still at school.'

'Ah.' Tess thought that explained a lot. 'Well, thank you for your insight. It was certainly—um—interesting.'

'And Marco's father?' prompted Silvio. 'You didn't say what he wanted.'

'Oh.' Tess had no intention of discussing the reasons for Castelli's visit with him. 'He—er—he was looking for Ashley.' She crossed her fingers. 'He didn't say why.'

'Mmm.'

Silvio didn't sound convinced, but Tess decided she had said enough. 'Now, I've got to go,' she said. 'I want to go to the supermarket before I go home.'

'Or you could have dinner with me,' Silvio suggested at once. 'There is a favourite *trattoria* of mine just a short way from here.'

'Oh, I don't think—'

'You are not going to turn me down?'

Silvio pulled a petulant face, but Tess had had enough. 'I am sure there are plenty of women only too eager to dine with you, Silvio,' she said firmly. 'I'm sorry, but it's been a long day and I'm tired. I wouldn't be very good company tonight.'

'But Ashley, she said you would be glad to go out with me,' he protested. 'She tell me you are not—attached, *no*?'

'Did she?' Tess wondered what else Ashley had told these people about her. 'Well, she was wrong, Silvio. I do have a boyfriend.' Boy*friends*, anyway, she justified herself. There was no need to tell him there was no special man in her life.

Silvio shrugged. 'But he is not here,' he pointed out blandly, and she sighed.

'Even so...'

'Another evening, perhaps,' he declared, evidently undeterred by her answer. Then to her relief he walked towards the door. *'A domani, cara. Arrivederci.'*

'Arrivederci,' she answered. 'Goodnight.'

Tess waited only until he'd stepped out of the gallery before shutting and locking the door behind him. Then, leaning back against it, she blew out a relieved breath. What a day, she thought. First Castelli, and then Silvio. She would be glad to get back to the apartment. At least there she could be reasonably sure she wouldn't be disturbed. Unless Ashley had some other secret she hadn't bothered to share with her sister, that was.

She slept badly, having only picked at the salad she'd prepared for herself. She kept thinking she could hear a phone ringing, but it was only the wind chimes hanging on the balcony outside the bedroom window.

In the event, she dropped into a fitful slumber just before dawn and when she woke again it was daylight and the sun was filtering through the blinds.

After putting on a pot of coffee, she went and took a shower in the tiny bathroom. The water was never hot, but for once she appreciated its lukewarm spray. She even turned the tap to cold before stepping out and wrapping herself in one of the skimpy towels Ashley had provided.

After pouring herself a delicious mug of black coffee, she stepped out onto the tiny balcony. The world looked a little less hostile this morning, she thought. But that was ridiculous, really. It was people who were hostile, not the world in general. And if anyone was to blame for her present situation, it was Ashley.

Her sister's apartment was on the top floor of a villa in the Via San Giovanni. The road was one of several that climbed the hill above the harbour, and, although the building was rather unprepossessing on the outside, at least its halls and stairways were clean and didn't smell of the onions and garlic that so many old buildings did.

Ashley's apartment was fairly spartan, but it was comfortable enough. She had added rugs and throws and pretty curtains at the narrow windows, and Tess had been pleasantly surprised to find it had a separate bedroom and bathroom as well as a living-room-cum-kitchen with modern appliances.

Now as she leaned on the balcony rail she amended the feelings of betrayal she had had the night before. Okay, Ashley had lied to her—had lied to all of them—but from Tess's point of view nothing had really changed. She was still filling in at the gallery and she had only herself to blame if she didn't enjoy the novelty of a break in such beautiful surroundings.

But it was hard not to wonder what Ashley was doing. Getting involved with a teenager seemed crazy, even by her sister's standards. Yet Ashley had always been a law unto herself. Tess could remember her father grumbling about his younger daughter's antics on one of his infrequent visits to Derbyshire to see her. He and his new family had still lived in London, but Tess had moved away when she'd become a teacher. It had been easier not to have to make excuses for not visiting her family as often as her father would have liked.

Realising her mug was empty now and that she was just wasting time, Tess turned back into the bedroom. Shedding the towel onto the rail in the bathroom, she walked naked into the bedroom again to find something suitable to wear.

Ignoring the suspicion that Raphael di Castelli's visit the previous day was influencing her, she chose a cream chemise dress that was spotted with sprigs of lavender. It was long, as her skirt had been, but she chose canvas loafers instead of the boots she'd worn the day before.

Her hair had dried in the sunshine and she surveyed its wisps and curls with a resigned eye. Some women might appreciate its youthful ingenuousness, but she didn't. She should have left it long, she thought gloomily. At least then she could have swept it up on top of her head.

Shrugging off these thoughts, she rinsed her coffee mug, left it on the drainer, and exited the apartment. Three flights of stone stairs led down to the ground floor and she emerged into the warm air with a growing feeling of well-being. She wasn't going to let Ashley—or Castelli—spoil her holiday, she decided. She had a good mind to shut the gallery early and spend the latter half of the afternoon on the beach.

Ashley's little Renault was parked a few metres down from the apartment building and it took some patience to extricate it from between a badly parked Fiat and a bulky van. It didn't help that she had to keep control of the vehicle by using the handbrake, the steep slope of the road making any kind of manoeuvre an act of faith.

She managed to regain her composure driving down to the gallery. Tumbling blossoms on sun-baked walls, red-and-ochre-tiled roofs dropping away towards the waterfront, buildings that seemed to be crammed so closely together, there didn't seem to be room for anything between. But there were gardens lush with greenery, fruit trees espaliered against crumbling brickwork. And the sensual fragrance of lilies and roses and jasmine, mingling with the aromas from the bakery on the corner.

The phone was ringing when she let herself into the gallery. Ashley, she thought eagerly, hurriedly turning off the alarm as she went to answer it. 'Hello?'

'Teresa?' Her spirits dropped. She should have known. It was Ashley's mother again. 'Teresa, where have you been? I've been trying the apartment but you weren't there.'

'I expect I was on my way down here,' said Tess, adopting a pleasant tone even though she felt like screaming. Then, with sudden optimism, 'Have you heard from Ashley?'

'No.' The clipped word conveyed it all, both distress and impatience. 'Have you?'

'If I had I'd have let you know,' said Tess flatly, and heard Andrea inhale a sharp breath.

'As would I, Teresa,' she said. 'And there is no need for you to take that tone with me. If you don't know where your sister is, I consider that's your mistake, not mine.'

Tess bit back the indignant retort that sprang to her lips. It was no use falling out with Ashley's mother. She was upset, and who could blame her? Her daughter had gone missing and she was over a thousand miles away.

'I suppose I assumed she'd keep in touch,' she said at last, deciding she didn't deserve to shoulder all the blame. 'And I did speak to her a few days ago.'

Andrea snorted. 'You didn't tell me that yesterday.'

Tess sighed. 'I forgot.'

'Or you kept it from me, just to worry me,' Ashley's mother said accusingly. 'Didn't you ask her where she was?'

No. Why should she? But Tess kept that question to herself.

'I never thought of it,' she said, which was true enough. 'Anyway, she'll be in touch again, I know, when she finds the time.'

'Well, I think it's a very unsatisfactory state of affairs,' declared Andrea tersely. 'And if it wasn't for this customer of Ashley's wanting to speak to her, I'd have heard nothing about it.'

Nor would she, thought Tess ruefully. But that was another story.

There was an awkward silence then, and before Tess could think of anything to fill it Ashley's mother spoke again. 'You know,' she said, 'I'm getting the distinct impression that you know more about this than you're letting on. And if Ashley was forced to ask you to stand in for her, she must have been desperate.'

Gee, thanks!

Tess refused to respond to that and Andrea continued doggedly, 'Well, all I can do is leave it with you for the present. But if you haven't heard from her by the end of the week, I intend to come out to Italy and see what's going on for myself.'

Tess stifled an inward groan. 'That's your decision, of course.'

'Yes, it is.' Andrea had obviously expected an argument and Tess's answer had left her with little more to say. 'All right, then. So, the minute you hear from Ashley, you'll ring me? You promise?'

'Of course.'

Somehow Tess got off the phone without telling the other woman exactly what she really thought of Ashley's behaviour. And then, after hanging up, she spent several minutes staring gloomily into space. She no longer felt like closing the gallery early and spending the rest of the day on the beach. This so-called holiday had suddenly become a trial of innocence and she was the accused.

It wasn't fair, she thought bitterly. It wasn't her fault Ashley had disappeared; it wasn't her fault that she had taken Castelli's son with her. So why was she beginning to feel that it was?

CHAPTER FOUR

SOMEHOW Tess got through the rest of the day. For once, she had several would-be customers in the gallery, and she spent some time talking to a couple from Manchester, England, who were visiting Italy for the first time.

Nevertheless, she was enormously relieved when it was time to close up. She returned to the apartment and another lonely evening feeling as if she were the only person in Porto San Michele who wasn't having any fun.

The next morning she felt marginally brighter. She'd slept reasonably well and, refusing to consider what would happen if Ashley didn't turn up, she dressed in pink cotton shorts and a sleeveless top that exposed her belly button. Why should she care what anyone thought of her appearance? she thought, slipping her feet into sandals that strapped around her ankle. This was her holiday and she meant to enjoy it.

With this in mind, she decided to give the car a miss this morning. A walk down to the gallery would enable her to pick up a warm, custard-filled pastry at the bakery, and the exercise would do her good. Italian food was delicious, but it was also very rich.

It was another beautiful morning. Outside the sun was shining, which couldn't help but make her feel optimistic. Whatever else Ashley had done, she had introduced her to this almost untouched corner of Tuscany, and she had to remember that.

Several people called a greeting as she made her way down the steep slope into town. She didn't always under-stand what they said, but she usually managed an adequate response. Her Italian was improving in leaps and bounds, and before all this business with Ashley had erupted she'd been happily planning a return to the country, maybe taking in Florence and Venice next time.

The pastry she'd bought at the small *pasticceria* was oozing custard onto her fingers as she let herself into the gallery. The alarm started its usual whine and she hurried to deactivate it before opening up the office and setting her backpack down on the desk. Then, before she had time to fill the coffee-pot, the telephone rang again.

Dammit, she thought, she couldn't get through the door before someone wanted to speak to her. Depositing the sticky pastry onto the notepad beside the phone, she picked up the receiver. 'Medici Galleria,' she said, expecting the worst.

'Miss Daniels?'

Tess swallowed. She would have recognised his distinctive voice anywhere. 'Signor di Castelli,' she said politely. 'What can I do for you?' Her heart skipped a beat. 'Have you heard from your son?'

'Ah, no.' His sigh was audible. 'I gather you have not heard from your sister either.'

'No.' Tess's excitement subsided. 'Nor has her mother.'

'I see.' He paused. 'You have heard from her?'

'Oh, yes. I've heard from Andrea.'

Tess couldn't keep the bitterness out of her voice and Castelli picked up on it. 'You sound depressed, *cara*,' he murmured sympathetically. 'Ashley's mother—she blames you, *sì*?'

'How did you know?' said Tess ruefully. 'Yes, she blames me. I should have asked Ashley where she was going when I spoke to her before I left England.'

'But you thought she was going to visit with her mama, *no*?'

'Andrea doesn't see it that way. In any case, I couldn't tell her what Ashley had told me.'

'*Povero* Tess,' he said gently. 'This has not been easy for you.'

'No.' Tess felt a momentary twinge of self-pity. 'So—' she tried to be practical '—was that the only reason you rang? To ask whether I'd heard from Ashley?'

'Among other things,' he said, rather enigmatically. Then, without explaining what he meant, *'Ci vediamo, cara,'* and he rang off.

Tess replaced the receiver with a feeling of defeat. So much for his sympathy, she thought gloomily. For a moment there, she'd thought he was going to offer some other alternative to her dilemma, but like Andrea he had no easy solutions. And, unlike Andrea, he had more important things to concern him than her situation, even if the two things were linked.

The pastry had oozed all over the notepad and she regarded it resignedly. So much for her breakfast, she thought, pouring water into the coffee maker and switching it on. Pretty soon the sound of the water filtering through the grains filled the small office, and the delicious smell of coffee was a temporary antidote to her depression.

Realising she still hadn't opened up the gallery, she went through into the studio and unlocked the door. Sunlight streamed into the gallery, causing her to wince at its brilliance, but everything looked brighter in the healing warmth of the sun.

Already the parade outside was quite busy. Cars and tourist buses surged past, looking for parking spaces along the popular esplanade. There were tourists and local fishermen leaning on the seawall across the street, and beyond the beach several yachts could be seen tacking across the bay.

They were heading for the small marina south of town and Tess envied them. There was something so exciting about being able to do whatever you liked on such a lovely day. With worrying about her sister, she'd almost forgotten what it was like to feel carefree, and her plan to loaf on the beach seemed far out of her reach today.

She stood for several minutes at the door of the gallery, watching the activities outside, trying not to feel too let-down. She didn't want to think of what she'd do if Ashley hadn't turned up by Friday. The prospect of her stepmother flying out here to join the search didn't bear thinking about.

There was a windsurfer out on the water. He had seemed fairly competent at first, but now she revised her opinion. He was probably a holiday-maker, she decided, trying his hand at sailing the narrow surfboard across the bay. And when an errant breeze caught the craft, he wobbled violently before overbalancing and tumbling head-first into the water.

To her relief, his head bobbed up almost instantly beside the capsized craft, but he couldn't seem to pull it upright again. She'd seen the experts do it, vaulting onto the board and pulling up the sail, but this poor man could only drift helplessly towards shallower water.

Tess couldn't suppress a giggle. Everyone on the beach and leaning on the seawall was enjoying his predicament. It wasn't kind to laugh, but she couldn't help herself. It was such a relief after the pressures she'd endured.

'You seem happier, *signorina*,' mused a low voice, and Tess turned her head to find Raphael di Castelli propped against the wall beside the door. His dark-complexioned features seemed absurdly familiar to her and she chided herself for the flicker of awareness that accompanied the thought.

'Signor di Castelli,' she said, knowing she sounded stiff and unwelcoming, but she hadn't expected to see him again so soon. 'You didn't say you were coming to the gallery today.'

'It was a sudden impulse,' he said, straightening away from the wall, and she was instantly intimidated by his compelling appearance. He was dressed less formally this morning, though his black trousers and matching silk jacket were no less exclusive in design. Still, he wasn't wearing a tie, she noticed, even if the dark curls of hair nestling in the open neckline of his black shirt provided a disturbing focus. 'And who told you my name was *di* Castelli? Have you spoken to Ashley, after all?'

'No, I haven't.' Tess was defensive now, backing into the

gallery behind her, allowing him to fill the doorway as he followed her inside. Married men shouldn't be so attractive, she thought, wishing she could be more objective. She didn't want to prove that she was no better than her sister, wanting something—or someone—she could never have. 'Besides,' she added, striving for indifference, 'that is your name, isn't it?' She paused and then went on defiantly, 'I'm told you're quite a celebrity around here.'

His eyes narrowed. It was obvious he didn't like the idea that she had been discussing him with someone else. 'Is that what your informant told you?' he asked. 'I think he is mistaken. Or perhaps you misunderstood.'

'I don't think so.' Tess moved hurriedly to open the blinds, anything to dispel the pull of attraction that being alone in a darkened room with him engendered. She moistened her lips. 'Did you forget something?'

Castelli arched a mocking brow. It seemed obvious that, unlike her, he had had plenty of experience with the opposite sex. And, just because he was married, he couldn't help amusing himself at her expense. He must know from her attitude that she didn't want him there, yet he seemed to get some satisfaction from her unease.

'As a matter of fact, I was on my way to Viareggio when I saw you standing in the doorway,' he declared at last, tracking her with his eyes as she moved around the room. 'You looked—*triste*.' Sad.

Tess caught her breath. 'You don't need to feel sorry for me, Signor di Castelli,' she said sharply, resenting his implication. 'I was just wasting time, actually. While I waited for my coffee to heat.'

Castelli regarded her indulgently. 'If you say so, *cara*,' he said. 'But I know what I saw in your face.'

Tess stiffened. 'Actually, I was watching a windsurfer,' she said. 'He made me laugh. Perhaps you mistook my expression for your own.'

'Do not be so defensive, *cara*. It is natural that you should feel this—excursion—has not been as you planned.'

'You got that right,' said Tess, heading towards the office. 'Now, if you'll excuse me…'

If she'd hoped he would take the hint and go, she was wrong. As she was standing staring down at the unappetising remains of her breakfast a shadow fell across the desk.

'Come with me,' he said, startling her more by his words than by his appearance in the office. She looked up to see he had his hands bracing his weight at either side of the door.

His jacket had parted and she noticed his flat stomach and the way his belt was slung low over his hips. Taut muscles caused the buttons of his shirt to gape; tawny eyes, narrowed in sensual appraisal, caused heat to spread unchecked through every pore.

Realising she was gazing at him like some infatuated teenager, Tess dragged her eyes back to the congealing pastry on the desk. 'I can't,' she said, without even giving herself time to consider the invitation. He must have known she'd refuse or he'd never have offered, she assured herself. 'I'm sorry. But it was kind of you to ask.'

'Why?'

'Why—what?' she countered, prevaricating.

'Why can you not come with me?' he explained, enunciating each word as if she were an infant. 'It is a beautiful day, *no*?'

'No. That is, yes—' Tess knew she must seem stupid, but it wasn't her fault. He had no right to put her in such a position. 'It is a beautiful day, but I can't leave the gallery.'

Castelli's mouth flattened. 'Because Ashley asked you to be here?' he queried sardonically. '*Sì*, I can see you would feel it necessary to be loyal to her.'

Tess stiffened. 'There's no need to be sarcastic.' She paused. 'In any case, I have to be here in case she rings.'

Castelli straightened away from the door. 'You think she will ring?'

Tess shrugged. 'Maybe.'

'And maybe not,' said Castelli flatly. 'I have the feeling

your sister will not get in touch with you until she is ready to return.'

Tess had had the same feeling. She didn't want to admit it but it would be counter-productive for Ashley to contact her, particularly if she'd taken pains to keep her whereabouts a secret.

'Whatever,' she said now, glancing round for the box of tissues Ashley kept on the filing cabinet. Pulling a couple out, she started to tackle the curdling pastry. 'I promised to look after the gallery. That's all there is to it.'

Castelli shook his head, and then moving forward he took the sticky tissues from her hand. 'Let me,' he said, glancing sideways at her as he gathered the crumbling remains of the pastry together, and her nerves spiked at the automatic association her senses made of his words.

She wanted to protest, to tell him she was perfectly capable of cleaning up her own mess, but she didn't. Instead, she stood silently by while he tore several damaged pages from the notepad, wiped down the desk and dumped the lot into Ashley's waste bin.

'The domestic will empty it,' he said, when Tess looked at it a little anxiously. Then, indicating his hands, 'You have a bathroom, *sì*?'

Tess moved aside, pointing to the door that led into the small washroom, and presently she heard the sound of him rinsing his hands. He came back, drying his hands on a paper towel that he also dropped into the waste bin. Then, he propped his hips against the desk, folded his arms and said, 'Are you not going to offer me a cup of coffee for my trouble?'

Tess had forgotten all about the coffee simmering on the hob, but now she took a spare mug from the top of the filing cabinet and filled it carefully. Her hands weren't entirely steady, but she managed not to spill any, offering the mug to him as she said tightly, 'I don't have any milk or sugar.'

'Why spoil a good cup of coffee?' he countered smoothly, though she guessed he regretted his words when he tasted the bitter brew. 'Mmm.' He managed a polite smile, but he put his cup down rather quickly, she noticed. 'It has a—distinctive flavour, *no*?'

'It's stewed,' said Tess shortly, tempted to remind him that she hadn't asked him to join her in the first place. 'I'm sure you're used to much better.'

Castelli's mouth twitched. 'I am sure I am, too,' he said without modesty. 'If you will come out with me today I will prove it.'

She shook her head. 'I've told you, I can't.'

His strange, predator's eyes flared with impatience. 'Because you do not trust me, perhaps?'

'Trust has nothing to do with it,' she said, though he was right, she did know very little about him. Stepping back from the situation, she could see he might have a point.

'What, then?' He moved to the door and glanced into the gallery. 'You have no customers. I doubt anyone will be too disappointed if you close. It is hardly an active concern. That is why Scottolino is thinking of moving his interest to *Firenze*—ah, Florence.'

Recognising the name she'd seen on the top of invoices Ashley had typed, Tess realised he was talking about the gallery's owner. 'Mr Scottolino is moving out of San Michele?' she asked in surprise. 'Does Ashley know that, do you think?'

'I doubt it.' Castelli was dismissive. 'Augustin is not the kind of man to keep his employees appraised of his plans. Particularly when it will mean that your sister will be out of a job.'

Tess's lips pursed. 'And your enquiries—as you so politely put it—won't have flattered her reputation, no?'

Her sarcasm was obvious and Castelli spread his hands, palms upward. 'You do me an injustice, Tess. I am not your enemy.'

You're not my friend either, thought Tess dourly, but his use of her name caused another unwanted frisson of excitement to feather her spine. She'd expected him to have forgotten it, she realised. It was Ashley he was interested in, Ashley who was his focus. Yet when he said her name in that low attractive voice that was as smooth and dark as molasses, her brain scrambled helplessly and she could have melted on the floor at his feet.

Fortunately, he didn't know that, but she did and it annoyed her. In consequence, her tone was sharper than it might have been when she said, 'You didn't tell me how your son met Ashley. Considering the opinion you apparently have of the relationship, it seems an unlikely event.'

Castelli was silent for so long that she thought he wasn't going to answer her. *He doesn't want to tell me that Marco has ambitions to be a painter,* she thought smugly, feeling as if she'd got the upper hand for once.

But she was wrong.

'They met last September,' he conceded at last. 'At the *vendemmia,* the grape harvest. There is always a celebration when the grapes are ready to press. Someone must have invited your sister to the gathering. For one evening of the year we keep open house.'

Tess frowned. 'Then you must have met her, too.'

'As I told you, I am informed I did.' He shrugged. 'There were many people. I do not remember.'

Tess absorbed this. 'I assumed they'd met at the gallery. I understand Marco is interested in art.'

'Now where did you hear that?' Castelli's eyes were once again focussed on her. 'It seems you, too, have been making the enquiries, *cara.*' His lips curled. 'My son's—interest in painting came after meeting your sister. It was an excuse to visit the gallery, nothing more.'

'You sound very sure.'

Castelli shrugged. 'Marco has never shown any aptitude for art before. He is a science student. He has always been more interested in the reality of life as opposed to the ideal.'

'Ah, but wasn't it Jean Cocteau who called art "science in the flesh",' Tess pointed out triumphantly. 'And surely you can't deny that Leonardo da Vinci was a scientist, as well as being one of the most influential painters of all time?'

Castelli pulled a wry face. 'You are determined to win this argument, are you not?' he remarked ruefully. 'And when it comes to quotations from the classics, you obviously have the advantage. But, please, do not tell me that Marco's infatuation for your sister is, as Ruskin said, "the expression of one soul talking to another", because I do not believe it.'

Tess was taken aback by his knowledge, but not really surprised. Raphael di Castelli struck her as being a very intelligent man and, contrary to his declaration, she doubted she had any advantage over him. But she understood his feelings, understood that it must be a source of frustration to him that Ashley had caused such a rift between him and his son.

'I can't imagine what Ashley thinks she's doing,' she murmured now, half wistfully. 'Her mother thinks I should report her disappearance to the police.'

'La polizia?' He seemed taken aback. 'But this is not a criminal matter.'

'No.' Tess didn't know why but suddenly she wanted to reassure him. 'I've managed to persuade her that there's no need to involve the police at present.'

'Grazie.'

He was obviously relieved and, taking advantage of his momentary weakness, she said, 'I gather your investigator hasn't turned up any clues.'

'No.' He was resigned. 'He is still in Genova, checking the automobile rental agencies, as I believe I told you. So far, he has had no luck in tracing their whereabouts.'

Tess sighed. 'I'm sorry.' And she was. As much for him, she realised with some confusion, as for herself.

His expression softened. 'You are not getting a very favourable picture of my country, are you, Tess? Or perhaps I should say, of my family. Despite his youth I accept Marco is also to blame.'

She managed a smile. 'Thank you for saying that.'

'My pleasure.' His voice stroked her senses. Then, with gentle insistence, 'You are not at all like your sister, are you, little one?'

Despite his reference to her size, the sudden intimacy of his words couldn't be ignored and she seized on the first thing she could think of in response. 'You're sure they're in Genoa, *signore*?' she asked hurriedly. 'Is it a big city?'

'It is a very big city,' he said drily, 'and at this point I am not sure of anything.' A trace of weariness entered his voice. 'That is why I am going to Viareggio. Marco may have confided his plans to his sister.'

'To his sister? I didn't know he had a sister.'

And why should she? she thought foolishly. It wasn't as if Castelli had confided his family connections to her. But somehow she'd got it into her head that Marco was an only child. Or perhaps, she'd only hoped he was. If Castelli had more children, he was even further out of reach.

He was regarding her with mild speculation now and she wondered what was going on behind his polite façade. What was he thinking? That she'd been presumptuous to say what she had? Or that she had no right to question his private affairs?

'My daughter married at the end of last year,' he replied at last, apparently deciding she deserved an answer. 'Maria—that is her name—she and Carlo, her husband, own a small *albergo* in a village not far from the city.' He paused. 'If you come with me, you can meet her for yourself.'

Tess sucked in a breath. She hadn't expected him to repeat his invitation and now that he had she was unsettled again. She knew she should still say no. Closing the gallery would be irresponsible and reckless. How would his daughter feel if her father turned up with a strange woman? Pretty peeved, Tess was sure.

No, she couldn't do it. Even if the idea of taking off for the day was almost irresistible, she had to keep her head.

Italian men had a reputation for liking women and Castelli was a married man besides. She'd be mad to put herself into his hands.

'I'm sorry,' she said at last, feeling real regret as she voiced the words. 'I don't think your wife would approve.'

'My wife?' He gazed at her strangely. 'What does my wife have to do with my asking you to accompany me on this trip?'

'Well…' Tess's face felt as if it were burning. Put like that it did sound as if she was attributing motives to him he clearly didn't have. 'I just thought—that is, I'm sure the rest of your family will think it odd if you turn up with—with a strange woman.'

His mouth flattened. 'Ah, a beautiful woman, *cosi intendi*?' he remarked softly, and Tess felt as if she couldn't get enough air. A faint smile lightened his expression. 'You think my wife and my daughter would not approve of my friendship with the attractive sister of my son's *innamorata, no*?'

Tess had never felt more embarrassed in her life. 'We're hardly—friends, *signore*. I just meant—'

'I know what you meant, Tess,' he assured her smugly, and she felt as if she wanted to scream with frustration. 'Relax, *cara*. There is no conflict of interest. There is only my daughter. My wife and I live separate lives.'

Tess wasn't convinced. 'But she still lives in your house, yes?'

'She lives in my house, *no*,' he teased her mockingly. '*Sono divorziato*, Tess. We are divorced. Gina makes her home in New York.'

CHAPTER FIVE

SHE didn't look as if she believed him and Rafe acknowledged that divorce was still not a common thing in his country. Indeed, hadn't his own mother been horrified that he should consider such a thing? Catholics did not get divorced, she'd told him severely. Marriage vows were meant to last.

But Rafe couldn't believe that anyone should be condemned to spend their lives with someone who flouted their vows so freely. Who, he suspected, had only married him to escape the rigorous dictates of her elderly father.

'I'm sorry,' Tess said now, cupping the back of her neck with her hands and drawing his eyes to the rounded breasts pressing against her sleeveless top. 'It's really none of my business.'

'No.' He conceded the point because he realised he was behaving totally out of character for him. *Dio mio*, he was too old to be—what?—flirting with a girl who was almost young enough to be his daughter. Well, perhaps that was an exaggeration, he conceded. But he was forty-three. More than old enough to have more sense.

'Anyway,' she continued, evidently taking his response at face value, 'I mustn't keep you.' She forced a polite smile. 'Will you let me know if—if your daughter does know where they are?'

And Rafe felt his resolve faltering. Dammit, what was wrong with inviting her to go to Viareggio with him? It wasn't as if he had any ulterior motive for doing so. She was Ashley's sister. She deserved to know what was going on.

Yeah, right.

'I had thought you might like to question Maria yourself,' he said, ignoring his conscience. 'Can I not persuade you to change your mind?'

Her hands dropped to her sides then and the colour that had ebbed and flowed from her cheeks all the time she had been speaking to him deepened again. 'Oh—really,' she said, making a distracted gesture towards her outfit. 'I couldn't go out dressed like this.'

'Why not?' She looked perfectly fine to him, bare legs and all. *And when had he noticed them?* 'This is not a formal visit, *cara*. You must have considered that what you are wearing was good enough to come to work, *no*?'

Tess lifted her shoulders, once again attracting his attention, this time to the gap of creamy flesh that widened between her top and her shorts. 'I don't know,' she murmured uncertainly, but he could tell she was weakening. 'How long would I be away from the gallery.'

'Um—two hours.' *Or three!* Rafe was not altogether truthful. 'Does it matter? Which is more important, pleasing your sister's employer or finding Ashley?'

'Well—finding Ashley, of course.'

Rafe inclined his head. 'Then shall we go?' he said, knowing he was giving her no option, and with a nervous little shrug she obediently picked up her bag.

He'd parked the Ferrari in a no-waiting zone and he noticed how her eyes widened at his audacity. Or perhaps she was just impressed with the automobile, though he doubted it. He didn't know why, but he had the feeling that possessions didn't matter much to Tess Daniels. Which was a novelty.

'I suppose it would be worth more than a parking attendant's job to tow your car,' she remarked as she folded her legs into the front passenger seat and Rafe felt a momentary spurt of indignation. He didn't need her to remind him that the authorities often turned a blind eye to his indiscretions. But he doubted that any defence he made would enhance his reputation in her eyes, so he chose not to comment on it.

'Are you comfortable?' he asked instead, getting behind the wheel, and he was gratified to see that she looked embarrassed now.

'How could I not be?' she remarked at last as he started the powerful engine. 'This is a Ferrari, isn't it? I saw the horse on the bonnet.'

Rafe winced. 'It's a stallion,' he said drily, and then wished he'd kept his mouth shut when she said,

'Oh, yes. An Italian stallion. I'd forgotten.'

Rafe glanced in his mirror and then took his chance to pull out into the stream of traffic. But her mocking words still rankled and, ignoring the safer path, he said, with a definite edge to his voice, 'I hope that was not meant as a criticism.'

Her lips parted then, and she turned her head to look at him, wisps of white-blonde hair blowing about her face. 'I don't know what you mean,' she said, lifting a hand to tuck several strands behind her ear. And, although he was fairly sure she knew exactly what he'd meant, he chose not to argue with her.

'*Non importa.* It does not matter,' he declared, but he was intensely aware of her beside him. Aware of her bare arms only inches from his sleeve, aware of the way her shorts rode up her thighs, exposing a smooth length of slim leg. He took a breath. 'Do you know Viareggio, *signorina*?'

She hesitated and he wondered if she intended to pursue what he had said earlier. But eventually all she said was, 'I've never been to Italy before so all I know is Porto San Michele, I'm afraid. And my name is Tess. I know you haven't forgotten it. Or have I offended you and that's why you've suddenly become so—so formal?'

They were leaving the small town behind them now, the hilly environs above the harbour giving way to a coast road that wound its way south. But it wasn't of the elegant little seaport of Viareggio that Rafe was thinking. He was wondering how to answer her without compromising his fear that he was getting in too deep.

'You have not offended me,' he told her neutrally. 'I do not offend that easily. But perhaps you are right. We do not know one another very well.'

The look she cast his way now was wary. 'So why did you invite me to come with you?' she asked, and Rafe's fingers tightened on the wheel.

Good question, he thought drily. But…

'You know why I invited you to come with me,' he said firmly. 'So you could talk to Maria yourself.'

'Mmm.' She didn't sound convinced. 'You think my presence will encourage her to talk? If she knows anything, that is?'

'I do not know.' He didn't like the feeling of being on the spot. 'But as this is your first visit to Italy, perhaps you will enjoy seeing a little more of my country.'

Tess gave him an undisguisedly disbelieving stare. 'But you didn't know it was my first visit to Italy until I said so,' she pointed out mildly, and Rafe expelled an impatient breath.

'No,' he conceded flatly. 'You win. I wanted your company.' His lips twisted. 'So sue me.'

Tess's jaw dropped. 'You wanted *my* company?' she echoed. 'Why?'

Were it anyone else, he might have been tempted to wonder if she was fishing for compliments. But not with Tess. There was such a look of perplexity on her face that he couldn't hide the humour that was surely evident in his eyes.

'I don't know any more about Ashley's whereabouts than I've already told you,' she continued, misinterpreting his expression. 'I want to find her just as much as you do. And if you think—'

'I believe you, *cara*,' he interrupted her gently. 'I know you have not been lying to me.' And then, because he wanted to wipe the suspicious look off her face, he added, 'Why should I not enjoy being with a younger woman? Just because I am over forty does not mean I am—what is it you say?—over the hill, *no*?'

Her eyes widened for a moment. Then she shook her head. 'I think you're teasing me, *signore*. It's kind of you, but I wish you wouldn't. I know my own limitations better than anyone.'

His eyes narrowed. 'And they are?'

Her colour deepened. With her face free of any obvious make-up and her hair blowing wildly about her head, she looked little more than a teenager, and he marvelled anew that she was older than her sister. From Verdicci's description, he knew Ashley Daniels was far more sophisticated— and comparably more worldly. She knew what she wanted and went after it, no matter who got hurt in the process. Including her own sister, he acknowledged as Tess moved a little uneasily in her seat.

'They're too many to mention,' she said at last, shifting her attention to the view. 'Oh, is that a monastery over there?'

Rafe decided to let her divert him, taking his eyes briefly from the twisting road ahead of them. A green rolling landscape, dotted with pine and olive groves, rose steadily inland. There were isolated farms, some of them with their own vineyards, and small villages visible among the trees. Some farmers grew vines between the olive trees, providing a much-needed boost to their economy in years when the grape harvest was poor.

Each village sported its own spire or *campanile,* and, hearing the distant sound of bells, Rafe guessed that was what Tess had heard, too. 'I think it is a church,' he said, returning his attention to the road. 'There are few monasteries surviving in this area. There are ruins, *naturalmente*, if you are interested. But I fear the thought of the noble priests does not inspire any enthusiasm in me.'

Tess frowned. 'Because you are divorced?' she asked innocently, and he smiled.

'No.' He cast a fleeting glance her way, once again

amused by her refreshing candour. 'I do not think I can blame them for that.'

'Then why—?'

'I was taught by the Jesuits,' he said. 'Who as you may know are not known for their *misericordia*—their mercy, *no*?' He paused reminiscently. 'It is a long time ago, but I have not forgotten.'

Tess seemed interested. 'You went to school here, in Tuscany?'

'No.' Rafe shook his head. 'I went to school in Rome.' He grimaced. 'My mother's greatest wish was that I should enter the priesthood.'

Her lips parted. 'The priesthood?'

'Unlikely, is it not? Is that what you are thinking? That this man who has been married and divorced should have been considered worthy of such an office?'

'No.' She spread her hands. 'I was surprised, that's all. I've never met a would-be priest before.'

'And I was never a would-be priest,' he assured her drily. 'That was my mother's dream, not mine. Fortunately my father was of a more practical persuasion. While he indulged her to the extent of allowing her to choose my source of education, I was his only son. It was necessary that I should inherit the vineyard, that I was able to take over from him when his health began to fail.'

'Is your father still alive?'

'No.' He spoke regretfully. 'He died almost twenty years ago.'

'He must have been very young.'

'He was fifty,' acknowledged Rafe ruefully. 'But he had always been a heavy smoker, *cara*. He knew the risks he was taking, but he could not shake the habit.'

Tess nodded. 'My father's dead, too,' she said, confirming something he had already suspected. 'He died of a heart attack last year.'

'Ah.' Rafe was silent for a moment and then he said, 'Do you miss him?'

'Not as much as I would have done if we'd lived together,' she admitted honestly. 'As I believe I told you before, I was brought up by my aunt when my mother died. Then, after college when I started teaching, I moved to another part of the country. Dad and I used to see each other from time to time, but it was never the same.'

'I get the feeling that your stepmother has a lot to answer for,' said Rafe drily. 'I suspect she is more like her daughter than you thought.'

'Oh, Andrea's all right.' Tess was instantly defensive of her family and he had to admire her for it. 'She only ever wanted one child. She hadn't bargained for two.'

'But she must have known your father was a single parent before she married him,' Rafe pointed out reasonably as Tess made a play of examining an insect that had landed on her bare leg.

'Is this a mosquito?' she asked, deliberately creating a diversion, and Rafe had stretched across and flicked it away before he gave himself time to think.

It wasn't until his hand was safely back on the steering wheel and his fingertips were registering the soft brush of her flesh that he realised what he had done. This wasn't his daughter, he reminded himself. She wasn't even his cousin. Tess was a virtual stranger and he was treating her like a friend. Or more than a friend, he conceded, his skin burning where he had touched her. And he wanted to touch her again, he thought, in places that were hot and wet and definitely forbidden.

As if she sensed his guilty attraction, Tess turned away from him now, pressing against the door beside her, keeping her eyes on the view. But only after they'd exchanged one searing look of raw intimacy that left Rafe at least stunned by the strength of his own response.

They were silent then, each of them occupied with their own thoughts, pretending an interest in their surroundings that Rafe was sure neither of them really felt. Or perhaps he was only imagining it, he thought irritably. Whatever, he was much too old to play these childish games.

Only there was nothing childish about the way he was feeling and, realising he had to normalise the situation, he was relieved when a cluster of villas strung out along the coastline came into view. 'This is Viali,' he said, trying to recover his earlier optimism. 'It is really just an extension of Viareggio these days. The port has expanded so much. But Viali is pretty. It has its own personality. And, although it cannot boast the art nouveau architecture for which Viareggio is famous, many people prefer it to the larger resort.'

'Is this where your daughter lives?' asked Tess, apparently prepared to meet him halfway, and he agreed that it was.

'Their *albergo* is situated just outside Viali on the way to Viareggio. They will not have too many guests at this time of the year. Maria should have plenty of time to speak with us.'

The Villa Puccini looked chic and elegant dreaming in the noonday sun. Lush vegetation provided a colourful backdrop to the warm cream walls of the villa, and the blue waters of a kidney-shaped swimming pool vied with the vast expanse of the Gulf of Genoa that lapped at the sandy shore below the gardens. Glancing at Tess's face, Rafe suspected it was far more attractive than she had expected, and he felt his own spirits lifting at more than the prospect of seeing his daughter again.

'Is this it?' Tess asked as he drove between the stone gateposts that marked the entrance to the drive, and Rafe blew out a breath. 'Do you like it?' he asked, slowing to avoid a group of holiday-makers who were heading into town. 'Carlo's family is heavily involved in the leisure industry. This is one of their smaller properties and the first one Carlo has managed alone.'

'One of the smaller properties,' echoed Tess disbelievingly. 'It's much larger than I expected. I thought an *albergo* was something like a bed-and-breakfast back home.'

Rafe gave her a brief smile. 'I think you are thinking of a French *auberge*, Tess,' he said, his use of her name coming far too easily. 'An *albergo* is a hotel. Sometimes large, sometimes small. The Villa Puccini falls some way between the two.'

Tess shook her head as they rounded a flowering trellis and a cluster of orange-tiled buildings came into view. It was obvious that the villa had been added to over the years. Some extensions were taller than others. But the overall effect was charming, set as it was beside the breathtaking beauty of the bay.

'It looks very impressive to me,' she said doubtfully, and he saw her give another anxious glance towards her bare legs.

'It is a holiday hotel,' he assured her gently. 'And you look exactly like one of the visitors.' He switched off the engine of the Ferrari and unfastened his seat belt. 'I intend to get rid of this jacket as soon as I am out of the car.'

She didn't look entirely convinced and, now they were here, Rafe had to admit to feeling a little apprehensive himself. It was the first time he had brought a young woman to his daughter's home, and, no matter how often he assured himself that his motives were innocent, the fact remained there had been no need for him to bring Tess along.

She unfastened her own seat belt now, and before he could forestall her she had pushed open her door and got out of the car. With the sunlight blazing down on her bare head and the flush of heat in her cheeks, she looked absurdly young and beautiful. As he shed his jacket and hooked it over his shoulder, he had to accept that Maria would be suspicious. It was not that she hadn't been urging him to find someone else for the past six years. It was just that this gamine slip of an English girl was unlikely to have been what she meant.

But, before he could marshal any arguments in his own

defence, he heard his daughter calling to him. She was coming from the direction of the gardens, a flat basket containing long stems of white and yellow blossoms draped across her arm. Maria's hair, which was as dark as his own but much longer, was confined in a single braid, and her chemise dress of simple white organza complemented the warm tan of her bare arms.

She looked as elegant as her surroundings, he thought, with a rueful sigh. A product of his mother's policy that a woman should always look her best, whatever the circumstances. Even if she'd been gardening, which was highly unlikely in Maria's case. His daughter might enjoy arranging flowers, but she left the planting and the picking of them to someone else.

The contrast between her and Tess was marked. And it was obvious that neither of them appreciated the comparison. As she drew nearer he saw Maria's dark brows arch in polite inquiry, but Rafe could tell from her expression that, however pleased she might be to see him, she didn't care for him bringing a strange woman here without forewarning.

'Papa,' she greeted him warmly as he stepped forward to meet her, reaching up and bestowing light air kisses beside each of his cheeks in turn. But then, with a lightening turn of mood, she began reprovingly, *'Avresti dovuto dirmelo che—'*

'Inglese, Maria, per favore,' he interrupted her smoothly, turning to beckon Tess to join them. His eyes met hers briefly, and then he turned back to his daughter. 'Tess, this is my daughter, Maria. Maria, this is Tess Daniels. You may recall, her sister is at present looking after the Galleria Medici in San Michele.'

There was a moment when he thought Maria looked almost guilty. She obviously recognised the name, though she tried to hide her reaction from him. *'Buongiorno, signorina,'* she said, forgetting in her confusion that he had asked her to speak English. And then, rescuing herself, *'Scusi, Papa.*

Non ricordo. How do you do, Miss Daniels? Are you enjoying your holiday?'

'Tess is not on holiday,' Rafe asserted, before Tess could explain herself. After Maria's telling little response to his question, the last thing he wanted was for Tess to warn her of why they were here. 'She is standing in at the gallery while her sister is away,' he continued smoothly. He put a cautioning hand on Tess's shoulder, trying to ignore how aware of her he was. 'I hope you don't mind, *cara.* I invited her to come see a little more of the area.'

Maria's lips definitely tightened. 'You should have told us you were coming, Papa,' she declared, offering Tess a limp hand. She regarded the other woman warily now as she added, 'Is this your first visit to Italy, Miss Daniels?'

'I'm afraid so.' Tess was not without perception and Rafe knew she must be blaming him for bringing her here. 'And, please, call me Tess.' She glanced about her, her gaze flicking over Rafe's as she did so. And over his hand on her shoulder. 'This is a beautiful spot. Your father didn't tell me how delightful it would be.'

Maria softened, but she was watching them closely and Rafe was reluctantly obliged to remove his hand. '*Sì*, it is beautiful,' she agreed, with a momentary air of satisfaction. Then she looked at her father again. 'Are you staying for lunch, Papa, or is this just a brief visit?'

Rafe shrugged. 'We are not in any hurry, *cara*,' he said. 'But we are both hot and thirsty and a cool soda would be welcome. We can decide about lunch later, *no*?'

Maria looked as if she would have preferred some kind of explanation as to why they were here before she offered them any refreshment. He doubted she had bought his story about giving Tess a guided tour of the area. But courtesy demanded that she play the generous hostess and a thin smile appeared as she said, '*Ma certo*, Papa. Please, come with me. We can have drinks on the patio.'

CHAPTER SIX

CASTELLI'S daughter led them along a path between a clump of oak and cypress trees. There was the scent of pine and the unmistakable tang of the sea. And when they emerged onto a private sun terrace, Tess could see a handful of guests basking on the beach below the hotel. There were striped chairs and tilted awnings, pedalos lying dormant in the noonday heat. Some children were paddling in the shallows, searching for shells, while their parents stretched out on towels on the sand.

She hadn't been exaggerating when she'd told Maria it was a beautiful place. The small town of Viali occupied a curving headland and the cliffs that rose above it were thick with pine and spruce. The beach was deep, stretching out some distance towards the water, with gently rising dunes studded with flowering cactus and prickly pear.

The terrace Maria took them to was separated from the public areas by a trellis totally covered with flowering vines. A teak table and chairs were set beneath a pale green umbrella, and as they approached a girl of perhaps eighteen, dressed in the uniform of a maid, bustled out to see if there was anything she could get them.

Maria ordered refreshments, consulting her father before adding a bottle of Chianti to her request. Then, after handing the basket of flowers to the girl, she gestured to Tess to take a seat.

It was all very polite, very civilised, but Tess knew that Castelli's daughter had not been pleased to see her. Oh, she'd hid it well, due no doubt to her father's influence, but Maria obviously considered Tess's presence an intrusion.

And it was, thought Tess unhappily. She should never

have agreed to come with him. It wasn't as if this trip was going to achieve anything except highlight the immense gulf between his—and Marco's—lifestyle and that of herself and Ashley.

Unless that was what he had intended to do, she reflected, resting her elbows on the table and cupping her chin in her hands. Though what influence he thought she might have on her sister, she couldn't imagine. The whole situation just got more and more bizarre and this had to be the last time she let him make her decisions for her.

He had seated himself beside her now, dropping his jacket over the back of his chair and rolling back the sleeves of his shirt over his forearms. A lean brown-skinned arm, liberally sprinkled with dark hair, rested on the table only inches from her elbow and she quickly withdrew back into her chair.

She hadn't forgotten the brush of his fingers against her thigh or the disturbing weight of the hand that had rested so briefly on her shoulder moments before. It was stupid to think it, she knew, but there'd been something almost possessive about the way he'd gripped her bones. He'd probably only done it to stop her from blurting out why they were really here, but that hadn't prevented the unsettling feeling it had given her in her stomach.

Had Maria noticed? She had certainly observed Castelli's hand resting on her shoulder and she was bound to be speculating about the kind of relationship they had. *No relationship*, Tess tried to communicate silently. This visit was far more innocent than it appeared. Maria didn't have to worry that her father was having a midlife crisis over her.

The maid returned wheeling a trolley. From within its chilled cabinet she took a jug of freshly squeezed orange juice, another of what looked like lemonade, and a squat jug of fresh cream. Riding on top of the trolley was a pot of coffee and some hand-painted cups and saucers, as well as a dish of almond biscuits and the bottle of wine Castelli had requested.

There were glasses, too, and a cut-glass vase containing a newly picked red rose still not fully in bloom. The girl placed everything on the table along with a handful of scarlet napkins, taking the trouble to set everything out so that her mistress could have no complaint, Tess was sure.

'*Grazie*.'

It was Castelli who thanked her, his infrequent smile causing her to blush with obvious pleasure. But then, he had that ability, thought Tess ruefully, to make any woman feel as if she was important. She had to remember that, too. It wouldn't do for her to think that his interest in her was anything more than self-serving.

Yet there had been that moment in the car when they'd talked more easily. He'd told her a little about his childhood and she'd explained how she'd felt when her father had died. He was easy to talk to and for a little while she'd forgotten what she was doing there and where they were going. However when his questions had become too personal she'd made the mistake of using the insect that had settled on her leg as a distraction, and suddenly she'd been painfully aware of how naïve she was.

The way he'd looked at her then had been far from impersonal. There'd been that stillness in his gaze that she'd seen once before and a frankly sensual curve to his mouth. He'd looked at her as if he was assessing what kind of partner she'd make in bed, she thought uneasily. It had been a devastating assault on her senses that had left her feeling confused and shivery and distinctly weak.

Of course moments later she'd been sure she'd imagined it. He hadn't repeated the look. In fact, he'd spent the rest of the journey in virtual silence. It hadn't helped that she hadn't been able to think of anything to say either. All she'd done was withdraw into her corner as if having a man stare at her had scared her to death.

But it was foolish to be thinking about such things here with his daughter regarding her with obvious suspicion and Castelli himself near enough to touch. Oh, God, she thought, this was getting far too complicated. She didn't want any kind of involvement, with him or anyone else.

'So, Papa,' said Maria, when the maid had departed again. 'How did you get to know Miss—er—Tess?'

'Teresa,' Castelli corrected her shortly, and Tess could only imagine the warning look he cast his daughter and which caused Maria's face to darken with colour. 'We met at the Medici Gallery, *naturalmente*. I was looking for her sister and she was not there.'

'No?' Was that a slightly uncertain note she could hear in the younger girl's voice now? Tess wondered. Whatever, Maria evidently tried to appear only casually interested. 'I did not know you were acquainted with the gallery, Papa.'

'I am not.' Castelli was sharp and to the point. 'But your brother is, *capisce*?'

Maria's jaw dropped. 'Marco?' she echoed, and Tess wondered if she was only imagining the consternation in the girl's voice now. '*Ma perché? Prego*—but why?'

'You do not know, *cara*?' There was no mistaking the censure in Castelli's tone. 'Do not lie to me, Maria. You knew of Marco's sudden interest in painting. I have heard him discussing his aspirations with you.'

'Well, yes.' Maria lifted her shoulders defensively. 'But why should I associate his interest in painting with the Medici Gallery?'

Castelli's eyes narrowed. 'You tell me.'

Maria cast a malevolent look at Tess, clearly resenting her observance of this embarrassing scene. If she could, Tess would have left the table then, just as unhappy with the situation as Maria. But she was a stranger here. She didn't even know where the restrooms were. And she was supposed to be monitoring the girl's reactions too. Did she know where her brother was or didn't she?

'I do not know what you are talking about, Papa,' Maria said at last, reaching for the jug of fruit juice and pouring some rather jerkily into an ice-filled glass. Her hand was shaking, however, and she spilled some of the orange juice onto the table. She only just managed to stifle her irritation as she snatched at a napkin to mop it up. Then, turning to Tess, she arched her brows. 'Juice or coffee?'

'Juice is fine,' said Tess, not wanting to risk the chance of getting hot coffee spilled over her, deliberately or otherwise. 'Thanks.'

'Papa?'

Castelli shifted in his seat and, although she was supposed to be concentrating on their exchange, Tess flinched at the bump of his thigh against her hip. Despite her determination not to get involved with him, she couldn't help her instinctive reaction to the contact. His thigh was hard and warm and masculine, and she felt the heat his body generated spread across her abdomen and down into the moistening cleft between her legs.

She doubted he'd noticed what had happened. After all, what had happened? Just a careless brush of his leg against hers. If she was absurdly sensitive, that was her problem. Castelli was totally focussed on his daughter. She might as well not have been there.

He made an eloquent gesture now, as if having to decide what he wanted to drink was an annoying distraction. 'Chianti,' he said after a moment, nodding towards the bottle of wine the maid had left uncorked in the middle of the table. 'But you will not divert me, Maria. Marco is missing. If I find out you know where he is, I shall not forgive you.'

Maria gasped. 'What do you mean, Papa? Marco is missing? Has he run away?'

'Do not be melodramatic, Maria. I suspect you know perfectly well what is going on. But in case you have any doubts, let me enlighten you, *cara*. Your brother has gone away with Ashley Daniels, Tess's sister.'

Tess wasn't sure what Maria's reaction meant then. She was shocked, certainly, but whether that shock was the result of Marco's behaviour or because her father had found her out, it was impossible to judge.

'But—that cannot be,' she said at last, her voice a little

unsteady. 'You are saying that Marco has some interest in the woman who runs the Medici Gallery? That is ludicrous. She is far too old for him.'

Tess decided not to take offence at Maria's words. After all, she was right. Ashley was too old for Marco. They were all agreed on that. Of course, hearing the scorn in Maria's voice did make her feel ancient. But what of it? It didn't matter what Maria thought of her.

'You knew he was seeing her, *no*?'

Castelli was relentless, and Maria sighed. 'I knew he visited the gallery,' she admitted. 'But he visited a lot of galleries, Papa. He told me he was interested in art. Why should I suspect his visits to this woman's gallery meant anything more than the rest?'

'Because he told you?' suggested her father grimly. '*Vene*, Maria, I am not a fool. Marco tells you everything. If he was interested in this woman, he could not have kept it a secret from you.'

Maria looked tearful now. 'You have to believe me, Papa. Do you think I would have encouraged him to do something like this?'

'I am not saying you encouraged him,' retorted Castelli. 'I believe you are far too sensible for that. But I do think he mentioned his interest in this woman to you. To—what shall we say?—to brag about it, *force*? Did he tell you the kind of relationship they had?'

Maria sniffed. 'I do not believe it.'

'What do you not believe? That Marco could be infatuated with an older woman? Or that he would hide his true feelings from you?'

'That he could be so—so stupid!' exclaimed Maria, looking at Tess as if she were in some way to blame for this fiasco. '*Bene*, Papa, I knew that he admired this woman. But she is old. I assumed she would have more sense than to take his advances seriously.'

'*Basta!*' Castelli threw himself back in his chair, his frustration evident, and Tess shifted uncertainly as he cast an

impatient glance in her direction. 'At last we have the truth.
You knew of Marco's affair and you chose not to tell me.'

Maria stifled a sob. 'There was no affair, Papa. *Solo*—
just a silly infatuation. If Marco has gone away, you have
no reason to believe he has taken this woman with him.'

Castelli shook his head. 'We know they went together,
Maria. They boarded a plane to Milano several days ago—'

'*A plane!*'

'But when the plane landed in Milano, they were not on
board,' he continued. 'We suspect they disembarked at
Genova. I am still hoping you can tell us why.'

Maria's lips parted. 'Me, Papa?'

Castelli nodded. 'If you have any information, any information at all, I advise you give it to me now.'

'But I do not.' Groping for one of the napkins, Maria
broke down completely. With tears streaming down her
cheeks, she exclaimed, 'I have told you all I know, Papa. I
am as unhappy with the situation as you are.'

'*Veramente?*'

Her father did not sound sympathetic and Tess wished
again that she'd passed on this trip. This was a family matter
and her involvement was an intrusion. All right, she wanted
to know where Ashley was, but it wasn't the matter of life
and death it seemed to the Castellis.

With Rafe di Castelli seething beside her, she felt as if
she couldn't get enough air and, picking up her glass, she
gently eased away from the table. Crossing to the low wall
that marked the boundary of the patio, she took a sip of the
fruit juice, wishing she possessed the sense of well-being
that had seemed so attainable before she'd left England.
Now she was on edge, embarrassed, conscious that she was
in some small part responsible. If she hadn't agreed to stand
in for her, Ashley could never have planned this escapade.

The sound of footsteps caused her to turn in time to see
another man come out of the building behind them. Not as
tall as Castelli and obviously much younger, the man went
straight to Maria's side and pulled her up into his arms.

'*Amatissima,*' he exclaimed, gathering her close and gazing accusingly at her father. '*Che c'e, cara. Si sente male?*'

'There is nothing wrong with her, Carlo,' declared Castelli in English, rising impatiently to his feet to face the other man. 'She is upset because her brother has disappeared and she might have been able to stop him.'

Carlo. Tess remembered the name. This obviously was Maria's husband. But his father-in-law's words had brought a frown to his fair handsome features and, despite his concern, he drew back to regard his wife's tear-stained face.

'*E vero?*'

He asked her if it was true and Maria nodded unhappily. But before she could say anything in her own defence her father intervened.

'Let me introduce you to my companion, Carlo,' he said, indicating Tess. 'Her grasp of our language is not so great. That is why we are speaking in English. Tess, this is my son-in-law, Carlo Sholti. Carlo, this is Tess Daniels. Her sister is the woman Marco has become infatuated with.'

Tess remained by the low wall, offering the young man a polite smile in greeting. She had the feeling Carlo was as curious about her presence as his wife had been earlier. But, at this point in time, Tess considered that as immaterial as her participation in this trip.

'Marco has disappeared,' put in Maria, regaining her husband's attention. 'Papa says he has gone with that woman who runs the gallery in San Michele. He thinks I should have told him they were friendly. But I had no idea Marco would do something like this.'

Carlo pressed Maria back into her chair and then turned to face Castelli. 'What is this woman's sister doing here?' he demanded, in English this time. 'Does she not know where they have gone?'

'Obviously not,' said Castelli curtly, as if he resented the implication of complicity. 'And I invited Tess to accompany me. Do you have a problem with that, Carlo, or is this the usual way you treat unexpected guests?'

Now it was Carlo's turn to look embarrassed. *'Perdone, signorina,'* he said stiffly. 'I did not mean to be rude.'

'It doesn't matter,' mumbled Tess, wishing she could just leave them to it. 'I'm sorry we've upset your wife. We're just trying to find out where my sister and your brother-in-law have gone.'

'Neatly put,' remarked Castelli drily, and meeting his eyes Tess was again reminded of how disturbingly attractive he was. Even here, with his daughter and his son-in-law watching their every move, she was supremely conscious of his maleness. And the dark colours he wore accentuated it; gave him an energy and a feline power that couldn't help but stir her blood.

'No problem,' she said at last, when it became obvious everyone was waiting for her answer. She moistened her lips. 'I think we should be going now. I—well, I've got to get back to the gallery.'

She'd half expected an argument; half hoped for one, she acknowledged uneasily, not looking forward to the journey back to San Michele. Castelli, sociable, Castelli friendly, she could handle. But Castelli impatient, Castelli angry, even, was something else.

'I think you are right, *cara.*' He chose to agree with her and she wondered if he used the endearment deliberately. He must know his daughter would resent the apparent familiarity between them. He swallowed the wine in his glass and set it carelessly back on the table. 'Much as we would have liked to join you for lunch, Maria, I agree with Tess. We should be getting back.'

'But, Papa—'

'Not now, Maria.' He was polite, but firm. 'If you think of anything else, I am just at the other end of the phone, *no*?'

'You will let us know, as soon as you have any news?'

That was Carlo, and Castelli's lips flattened against his teeth. 'If I can return the request,' he said. 'Maria may remember something she has presently forgotten.'

Both Carlo and Maria came to see them off. Maria had dried her eyes now and looked more resentful than upset. She looked on sulkily as Castelli swung open Tess's door and waited for her to seat herself before closing it again. Once again, Tess was intensely conscious of her bare legs and of how provocative her appearance must seem to the younger woman.

But she couldn't do anything about it. She just hoped Maria didn't think she had designs on her father. However attracted she might be to him, she thought she was sensible enough to know he was far beyond her reach.

As they drove away Castelli seemed absorbed in his thoughts, and Tess was glad to relax after the tensions of the last hour. Nevertheless, she found herself replaying all that had been said and she wondered if Maria was doing the same.

'Do you think I was cruel?' he asked abruptly, and Tess marvelled that he should have guessed her thoughts so exactly. 'I can see you are troubled,' he went on wryly. 'I was not very sympathetic, was I?'

Tess hesitated a moment, then she said, 'No,' in a noncommittal voice. His relationship with his daughter was nothing to do with her and she wished he wouldn't behave as if it were.

'And how would you have handled it?' he inquired, his fingers flexing on the wheel. He had very masculine hands, broad yet long-fingered. She had a momentary image of those hands brown against her white body. Of how the blunt tips of his fingers would feel caressing her quivering flesh.

Dear God!

She was still fighting to dispel those feelings when he looked at her again and she realised he was waiting for her reply. 'Um—I don't know,' she muttered. 'It's nothing to do with me.' She tried to think positively to prevent the inevitable rejoinder. 'I—er—I think she was genuinely shocked about what had happened.'

'Oh, so do I,' he concurred drily. 'I am sure Maria is

upset because Marco did not confide his plans to her. But she is also jealous of your sister.' His tawny eyes swept over her appraisingly. 'She finds it hard to accept that her brother might have needs she cannot satisfy.'

Tess felt the insidious warmth spreading up from her throat and struggled to divert the conversation. She couldn't discuss his son's sexual needs with him! 'The—er—the *albergo* was very nice,' she said, smoothing her damp palms over the hem of her shorts. Then, realising he had noticed what she was doing, she tucked her hot hands between her knees. And because the adjective she'd used was so insipid, she added, 'It must be wonderful to live in such a lovely spot.'

'I am glad you liked it,' he said at last, and she wondered if the delay was a deliberate attempt to disconcert her. If so, it had worked. 'It is a pity you did not get the chance to see more.'

'I don't think your daughter would agree with you,' murmured Tess, almost without thinking, and Castelli's brows drew together as he absorbed her words. 'I mean, I don't think she was in the mood for visitors,' she added hastily. 'She hasn't been married very long. And she does seem very young.'

'Maria is nineteen,' he told her evenly. 'And I know exactly what you meant. You think my daughter did not approve of my bringing you with me.' He shifted in his seat. 'But like my son, I too have my own life to lead.'

Tess had no answer for that. Turning her head, she stared out blankly at the fields of waving poppies that stretched inland in a colourful swath. She saw a village clinging to the hillside, and tried to be objective. But how was she supposed to deal with him? The experiences she'd had in England, infrequent as they'd been, had not prepared her for his magnetism.

Pursing her lips, she decided not to let him faze her. She was a grown woman, for heaven's sake. Not some impressionable girl who was overawed because a man had paid some attention to her. 'I expect there are many women in your life, *signore*,' she said, with amazing nonchalance. 'Someone of your experience must be very much in demand.'

The breath he expelled then conveyed a mixture of admiration and humour. 'You think?' he murmured faintly. 'And call me Rafe, if you will. Not *signore*.' He paused. 'And now you have surprised me, *cara*. I am not sure whether that was a compliment or not.'

Call him *Rafe!* Tess swallowed. She could just imagine how Maria would feel about that. 'I was merely stating the obvious,' she said, managing to avoid calling him anything. 'If Maria objected to your companion today, it was not because she'd never seen you with a woman before.'

'No?'

'No.' Now she'd started, she had to finish, and Tess inhaled a deep breath. 'I'm just different from the usual women you have dealings with. Maria was resentful because—well, because of who I am.'

'Ashley's sister,' he said mildly and she sighed.

'That's the least of it and you know it.' She paused. 'I don't fit the image of the kind of woman you obviously prefer.'

He glanced her way then, and Tess was intensely conscious of the intimacy of his gaze. 'And that image would be?' he said, causing her no small measure of uneasiness. 'Come, Tess, you cannot say something like that without elaborating. So tell me. What kind of woman do you think I like?'

She bent her head in confusion. As usual, he was determined to have the last word. 'Someone more sophisticated; someone more elegant,' she muttered at last, lifting her hands and cupping the back of her neck almost defensively. Then, exasperated, 'How do I know? I'm just guessing that your companions don't usually wear shorts.'

The car slowed then and for a moment she thought he was stopping so that he could continue the argument more forcefully. But, instead, he pulled onto a gravelled headland overlooking the beach below. There was a van parked there, too, the kind that supplied snacks and sandwiches to weary travellers, and, after turning off the engine, he said, 'I think it is time for lunch, *no*?'

CHAPTER SEVEN

RAFE could see she was surprised by his choice of venue. It made him wish he had asked his housekeeper for a packed lunch that they could have eaten in more salubrious surroundings than this. But then, he hadn't known he was going to ask Tess to join him when he'd left the villa that morning, he reflected drily. That impulse, like the impulse he had now to comb his fingers through the silky tangle of her hair, was not something he should consider repeating.

Now, however, she looked at him out of the corners of those limpid green eyes of hers and he realised she had misread his intentions. 'Do you usually patronise sandwich bars, *signore*?' she asked tightly. 'Or do you gauge your eating habits according to the sophistication of your companion?'

Rafe pulled a wry face. 'You are offended because I have not taken you to an expensive restaurant?' he queried innocently, and saw the familiar colour darken her cheeks.

'You know that's not what I meant,' she declared hotly, pushing her back against her seat. 'But if you're only stopping because of me, don't bother. I rarely eat lunch anyway. I can wait until we get back to San Michele.'

'Well, I cannot,' he retorted, pushing open his door and getting out of the car. 'And contrary to popular supposition, plenty of good food can be found at roadside kiosks, *no*?'

'I can't see you eating a burger, *signore*,' said Tess, pushing open her own door and joining him. The brilliant noonday sun immediately burned on her uncovered head and shoulders, and she caught her breath. 'Goodness, it's hot!'

Rafe studied her bare arms with some concern. 'Perhaps

77

you should stay in the car,' he said, resisting the desire to smooth his fingers over her soft skin. 'It is cooler there.'

'What? And miss the chance to see what the chef has on offer?' she asked lightly, and his pulse quickened at the unexpected humour in her face.

'Okay.' He saw her looking at the curving line of the shoreline that fell away below the promontory. 'Let us get something to eat and drink and find somewhere more private to enjoy it, *no*?'

Tess caught her breath. 'You mean, go down to the beach?' she asked, viewing the precipitate descent with some concern. 'Isn't it too steep?'

'Do not tell me you are afraid of heights, *cara*.' He teased her mercilessly. 'Where is your sense of adventure?'

Tess shook her head. 'I don't think I have one, *signore*,' she murmured unhappily. 'But—if you can do it—'

'An old man like me, you mean?' he queried wryly, and she turned to give him an impatient look.

'You're not old, *signore*,' she protested, and he sighed at her continued use of the formal means of address.

'Then why do you persist in calling me *signore*?' he countered, his eyes intent on her flushed face. 'You know my name, Tess. Use it.'

'I—I don't think I should call you Rafe,' she exclaimed, and he had the impression that she found it difficult to drag her gaze away from his.

'Why not?'

He couldn't prevent himself from pursuing it and this time she succeeded in breaking the connection. 'Because— well, just because,' she mumbled lamely. Then, in an effort to divert him, she added, 'Oughtn't we to choose a sandwich or something? The owner will think we've just stopped here for the view.'

'Works for me,' murmured Rafe before he could stop himself, and she cast one astonished look in his direction before moving away towards the van.

Rafe was pleased to see that the man who ran the booth

was offering cheese-filled *panini* and steaming slices of pizza as well as the more common *tramezzini* or sandwiches. There were ready-made salads, too, in foil-wrapped containers, and spicy *bruschetta*, spread with olive or tomato paste.

It was obvious Tess didn't know what to choose, so he took it upon himself to place two orders for pizza and salad, and a slice each of *tiramisu* for dessert. Sealed cups of black coffee completed the meal and he was aware that Tess looked at him rather doubtfully as he carried his purchases back to the car.

'I—how do you propose to carry all that?' she asked, and he remembered that she still thought he intended to scale the cliff to reach the beach.

'You will see,' he said, opening the boot of the Ferrari and putting the bags and containers inside. He smiled to himself at the thought of what his mother would think of him—as she would put it—abusing the automobile in this way. Tess hadn't been far wrong. He wasn't in the habit of eating the food from roadside kiosks. But that was not to say he wasn't going to enjoy it this time.

Tess was frowning now, and circling the car, he swung open her door. 'Get in, *per favore*.'

Tess hesitated. 'I thought you said—'

'Just get in,' he urged her softly, and, although he could see the uncertainty in her face, she was too polite to refuse.

He watched as she swung her legs inside, assuring himself he was only waiting to close the door when in his heart of hearts he knew he had a more personal reason. He enjoyed watching her, enjoyed disconcerting her. However much he might regret his impetuosity tomorrow, for today he intended to live each minute as it came.

A moment later, he slid in beside her, instantly aware of the feminine aroma of her heated skin. It was a disturbing scent, unfamiliar and definitely sensual. It aroused him as nothing had that he could remember, and the urge to touch her was almost overwhelming.

But he controlled himself, consigning the insistent pull of attraction to the back of his mind. All right, he sensed she was aware of him, too, but she'd probably run a mile if he acted on it. Apart from anything else, they hardly knew one another. So why did he feel as if he'd known her for half his life?

Casting her a brief half-smile, he started the car and drove away from the headland. But not far. Just a few yards further on, a winding track almost overhung with wild bramble and juniper dipped away from the coastal road. Anyone who didn't know it was there would never have noticed it, particularly at this time of the year when the blossom was out.

He was aware that Tess had turned to stare at him now and he guessed what she was thinking before she spoke. 'You never had any intention of climbing down the cliff, did you?' she exclaimed, but her tone was more relieved than accusing. Then as the car swung round a hairpin bend she groped for the edge of her seat. 'Is this road going somewhere or are we likely to get stuck halfway down?'

'Relax, *cara*,' he said, taking a hand from the wheel to briefly touch her knee. 'I know what I am doing.'

But did he? he wondered as he withdrew from that strangely intimate connection. Once again, he had acted on impulse and now her gaze was decidedly uncertain as it darted away from his.

'I hope so,' she mumbled almost under her breath, but he heard her and chided himself for causing more tension between them. He'd intended this to be a light-hearted interlude before he returned her to Porto San Michele, but he was in danger of creating problems that might be far harder to deal with than Marco's boyish infatuation for her sister.

The track narrowed as it neared the bottom of the cliffs and he winced as the untamed bushes scraped along the sides of the car. A mistake in more ways than one, he thought ruefully, but that didn't stop him from feeling an ungovernable sense of anticipation at spending a little longer in Tess's company.

As he'd hoped, the shallow plateau above the beach was deserted. There was just room enough to turn the car and his satisfaction at their seclusion was only equalled by his relief that his memory of the place hadn't been faulty.

And it was just as beautiful as he remembered. The untouched stretch of beach was enclosed on either side by a rocky promontory, and the sand was as pure and untouched as when the cove was formed. At the shoreline, waves broke into rivulets of foam, and beyond the dazzling brilliance of the sea the sky rose, a cloudless arc of blue above. They could have been alone on some desert island were it not for the sails of a yacht heading far out towards the horizon.

Tess thrust open her door as soon as he stopped the car. Getting out, she walked to the edge of the turning area and lifted both hands to protect the top of her head. He wondered what she was thinking as she stared out to sea. He hoped she wasn't regretting coming with him. For the first time in more years than he cared to calculate, he was enjoying himself and he didn't want anything to spoil it.

But he had been sitting there too long watching her, and when she glanced back over her shoulder he saw the doubt in her eyes. He at once opened his door and, pushing his feet out onto the sun-baked earth, he crossed the space that divided them.

'I suppose you knew this was here,' she said as he joined her. Then, turning back to the view, she added somewhat wistfully, 'It is a marvellous place.'

'You like it?' He was pleased. 'Thankfully, it has not yet been discovered by the tourists.'

'Down that track?' A smile was in her voice. 'I dread to think what you've done to your car.'

'It is only a car,' he assured her mildly. 'If it needs a paint job, then so be it.'

Tess shook her head. 'You say that so casually. Most people have to take care of their possessions.'

Rafe sighed, realising he had been careless. 'Perhaps I measure my possessions differently, *cara*,' he said softly.

'People are more important to me than—what shall I say?—pretty toys, *no*?'

She shrugged and as she did so he noticed how the sun had already tinged the skin of her upper arms with a rosy glow. She would burn easily, he thought, the knowledge increasing the sense of protection he already felt towards her. He wanted to—

But, no. He was already getting ahead of himself and, turning back to the car, he collected the bags containing their lunch from the boot. 'Come,' he said, stepping into the tangle of reeds and grasses that bordered the plateau. 'We can have lunch in the shade of the cliffs, yes?'

'Okay.'

He saw her give another glance back towards the car before she followed him down onto the sand. Then, kicking off her shoes, she seemed to relax, and by the time he had spread his jacket for them to sit on she was right behind him.

'I know,' he said as she dropped her shoes beside her. 'This will not do my jacket any good either. But in this instance, it can be cleaned.'

'If you say so.'

Apparently deciding she had no choice than to trust him, she seated herself at the edge of the jacket, drawing up her knees and wrapping her arms about them. Rafe dropped down beside her, trying not to stare at the smooth flesh disappearing into the cuffs of her shorts. Imagining what lay beneath the pink cotton was not only unforgivable, it was stupid, and he distracted himself by opening the bags and containers and setting them out between them.

'What would you like to eat?' he asked, when Tess seemed to be more interested in the tiny shells that dotted the sand at her feet than the food. 'Salad? Pizza?'

'What? Oh—' He was suddenly sure she was only pretending not to have noticed what he'd been doing. 'Um—salad sounds good.'

He met her wary gaze with a deliberately neutral stare. 'Only salad?'

She shifted a little awkwardly. 'Well—maybe a slice of pizza, too,' she agreed, accepting the salad container from his hand. 'Thanks. This looks good.'

'I hope so.' He helped himself to a slice of the pizza and bit into it with feigned enthusiasm. The tomato juice oozed onto his chin and he grabbed a napkin to wipe it away. 'Hmm. *Molto bene.*'

'I'm sure you're only saying that,' she murmured, forking a curl of radicchio into her mouth. 'But it was kind of you to do this. I appreciate it.'

'I did not do it out of kindness.' Rafe was stung by the implication that there could be no other reason for him to want her company. He swallowed another mouthful of pizza, licking the melted cheese from his lips before continuing tersely, 'It is I who should thank you for accompanying me to Viali.'

Tess hesitated. 'I don't know why,' she said at last. 'It would have been easier for everyone if I hadn't been there.'

'I think we covered that some miles back.' Rafe was impatient. 'Can we not forget the reasons why we started out on this expedition and concentrate on the here and now? Are you not enjoying yourself, is that what all this is about?'

Tess cast a brief glance his way. 'All what?' she queried tensely and he blew out a weary breath.

'You know,' he told her flatly. 'Ever since we left the *albergo*, you have been as—as jumpy as a cat. What did I do? What have I said to upset you?'

'Nothing.'

The answer came far too quickly and Rafe thrust his pizza aside and got abruptly to his feet. 'If you would care to finish your salad in the car, we can leave immediately.'

'No.' That answer came quickly, too, but this time it was accompanied by an embarrassed glance at his face. 'Please, I didn't mean to annoy you. It's just—well, I'm sure there are places you'd much rather be than here.'

'And if there are not?'

Her tongue appeared between her teeth and he felt the sudden tightness in his loins as she wet her lips. 'You're sure you're not just saying that?'

'No.' He hunkered down beside her, one hand moving of its own accord to cup her cheek. He tilted her face to his. 'Believe me, *cara*, at this moment there is no place I would rather be than here.' His eyes darkened as they rested on her mouth. But only for a second. He was on dangerous ground, he realised, aware of what he really wanted to do. Withdrawing his hand abruptly, he got to his feet again, looking down at her. *'Bene,'* he said tensely. 'Enjoy the rest of your meal. I will not be long.'

Her eyes widened. 'Where are you going?'

Rafe stifled a groan. He wondered how she would react if he told her the truth. That he was desperate to put some space between them before he did something unforgivable. He didn't just want to stroke her cheek or make casual conversation as they'd done in the car. He wanted to put his tongue where hers had been a few moments ago, to cover her mouth with his and find a partial release of his frustration in a kiss.

'I thought I might take a walk,' he offered at last. 'I need to stretch my legs.' *And cool my libido.*

Tess's eyes moved from his constrained features to the undulating water and he glimpsed the wistful look that crossed her face. But, 'Okay,' was all she said and it was left to Rafe to feel a heel for behaving so callowly. He'd brought her here, *per amor di Dio*. It wasn't her fault that he couldn't control his rampant desires.

'Io—come with me. If you wish,' he said, before he could stop himself, and she sprang eagerly to her feet.

'You don't mind?' she asked, dropping the carton containing the remains of her salad onto the sand. He gave a faint smile of acquiescence. It seemed the decision had been made and he would have to live with it. It wasn't as if he wanted to leave her alone.

Tess left her shoes with the rest of their belongings, practically skipping across the sand to dip her toes in the cooler waters of the gulf. She shivered dramatically, laughing as the incoming tide swirled about her ankles. She was like a child, he thought ruefully. As natural and uninhibited as his own children had been before adolescence, and their mother's desertion, had had such an impact on all their lives.

'Oh, this is heavenly,' Tess said, linking her fingers together and stretching her arms above her head in obvious delight. 'Thank you so much for bringing me.'

'I am happy you are enjoying yourself,' he said politely, forcing himself not to linger. He was quite sure she was unaware of the effect she had on him but it was far too easy to imagine his hands circling that deliciously bare midriff as he tumbled her onto the sand.

Unknowingly, he had quickened his step and by the time he realised it and glanced over his shoulder Tess was some distance behind him. She was following much more slowly, splashing through the shallows, her delight in her surroundings apparently dissipated by his indifference. Once again he felt the familiar pangs of guilt. It wasn't fair of him to spoil the day for her.

Despite his reluctance, he waited for her to catch up with him, but now she wouldn't meet his gaze. She halted beside him, her eyes seemingly glued to the yacht that was now disappearing over the horizon. She had obviously sensed his ambivalence and misread the reasons for it.

'What is wrong?' he asked, as if he genuinely didn't know. 'It is very hot, is it not? Have you had enough?'

'Have you?'

Her retort caught him unawares and he didn't have an answer for her. 'It is—getting late,' he said lamely, although it was barely three o'clock. 'I would not want you to get burned.'

She lifted first one arm and then the other, looking at them as if she hadn't considered them before. But she didn't look convinced. Despite the fact that the skin of her shoulders looked slightly sore, she gave a careless shrug. 'Perhaps you're right,' she said without conviction. 'If it's what you want.'

Rafe stiffened. 'What I want does not signify.'

'Oh, I think it does.' He caught a glimpse of indignant green eyes, quickly averted. 'I should have realised before. When you said you were going for a walk. You didn't really want me to come with you, did you?'

'*Io*—' Rafe was nonplussed. He hadn't realised he had been so transparent. 'That is not true.'

'I don't believe you, *signore*.' She used the term deliberately, he was sure, and it infuriated him. 'All this—buying the food, bringing me down here—was just a way of appeasing your conscience.'

Rafe's jaw dropped. 'Appeasing my conscience?' he echoed, stung by the accusation. 'Why should I feel the need to appease my conscience? I have not done anything wrong.'

Yet.

'You feel as if you have,' said Tess doggedly, and for a moment he wondered if she'd read what he was thinking. He hoped not. And, to his relief, she seemed to confirm it. 'You think you've upset both your daughter and me,' she continued. 'So you decided to pacify one of us with a peace-offering. In this case, an hour of your precious time, right?'

'Wrong.' He was annoyed by the objectivity of her reasoning. Not least, because it was so far removed from the truth. 'When I invited you to have lunch with me, it was because I wanted to. Not for any other reason.'

'So why do you want to cut the afternoon short?' she asked impulsively. 'Am I keeping you from some important previous engagement?'

'No.' His breath gushed out in a rush. 'I am sorry if I have given you that impression.'

'Well, what else can I think when you seem determined to avoid me?' she countered, looking up at him now with a wary, uncertain gaze. 'You seem to—to blow hot and cold in equal measures. I—well, I don't know how you really feel.'

Rafe's good sense deserted him. 'I was not trying to avoid you,' he said huskily. 'If it seemed that I was—and I am admitting nothing, you understand?—perhaps it was because I find you far too—appealing, *no*?'

He'd shocked her now. He could see it in the face that she turned up to him. But, what the hell, he'd shocked himself, and that was far more disturbing.

'You don't mean that,' she said, and he knew that this was his last opportunity to escape the consequences of his outburst. He had only to tell her he was teasing and he might be able to get out of this unscathed.

But he didn't do it.

'I do mean it,' he said, the words coming even though his brain was trying desperately to silence him. 'You are—enchanting. And beautiful. And I would not be a man if I did not find you desirable, *mi amore*.'

Her lips parted then, and, although he sensed she was as uncertain of the good sense of what they were doing as he was, she didn't move away. Instead, she came a little nearer, her toes brushing the front of his loafers, those clear green eyes keenly searching his face. Almost involuntarily, it seemed, she lifted her hand and stroked the roughening skin of his jawline, and Rafe could no longer control the instinctive hardening between his legs.

'So—do you want to kiss me?' she breathed barely audibly, and the quicksands of passion moved beneath his feet.

'Tess—' he said hoarsely, and even then he thought he might have found the will to resist her. Yet when her hand dropped to the open neckline of his shirt and he felt those tentative fingers against his bare skin, he totally lost it. The groan he uttered was purely anguished, and his hands found her shoulders to haul her into his arms.

Her lips were already parted, inviting the hungry invasion of his tongue. He didn't disappoint her. One hand moved to grip her nape, angling her face towards him as his mouth

fastened greedily over hers. His kiss both enticed and seduced, drawing a response from her that sent his head spin-
ning. He felt his own gnawing hunger controlling his actions
as his senses whirled out of control.

Her arms wound around him, her palms spreading against
the damp curve of his spine. She must have been able to
feel the heavy weight of his erection throbbing against her
stomach but she didn't recoil from him. When his hand
cupped her buttocks, bringing her into intimate contact with
his arousal, she arched against him, letting him feel how
responsive she also was to his touch.

A sexy little moan emerged from lips that were already
wet and swollen from his kisses and his conscience resur-
faced. *Dio mio*, he thought, if he didn't stop this soon he
would go all the way. He was in real danger of acting out
the images that had been taunting him all morning, and
while he couldn't deny he wanted her, she was simply not
for him.

She was too young, for one thing, and she probably saw
this as just a pleasant adjunct to her holiday. She'd had a
tough time of it so far, what with Ashley's disappearance
and her stepmother breathing down her neck. Not to mention his own less-than-subtle hints about what he thought of
her family. He wasn't conceited, but he could quite see that
having him lusting after her might offer some compensation.
Particularly if, as seemed likely, she had little experience
with older men.

His own feelings were less straightforward. And however
tempting making love with her might be, he still had enough
sense to step back from the ultimate betrayal. He could do
without any more complications in his life, he thought cyn-
ically. From his point of view, it would be a recipe for
disaster.

Which was why, when he lifted his mouth from hers, he
didn't succumb to the urge to slide his hands beneath the
hem of her tank top and let his thumbs caress the undersides
of her breasts. He wanted to. *Dio*, he wanted to feel her pert

nipples taut against his palms and to take those firm mounds of flesh into his hands. Instead, stifling a groan, he gripped her forearms and put her gently away from him, feeling every kind of a heel for having led her on in the first place.

Her confusion was obvious and he couldn't blame her. He hadn't been able to hide his body's reaction to her and in her book there was probably only one conclusion to this affair. But when he met her troubled gaze with eyes that were deliberately regretful, she soon got the message. She took a stumbling backward step before turning and hurrying away along the beach.

'*Cara!*' He couldn't use her name, that would be too familiar. '*Cara,*' he called again. 'I am sorry. I do not know what came over me.'

She muttered something then, but she was too far away for him to hear it. But he could imagine it wouldn't be complimentary and who could blame her? He had behaved abominably and she deserved so much better. She was bound to think he had as little respect for her as he had for her sister.

CHAPTER EIGHT

THE wind chimes woke her.

Tess had thought that she wouldn't sleep, but surprisingly enough she'd fallen into a deep slumber as soon as her head touched the pillow. Perhaps it had been the heat or the tiring quality of the journey, she mused, rolling onto her back and staring up at the dust motes dancing in the rays of sun seeping through the blinds into the bedroom. Or more likely it had been the stress, she thought bitterly, as the remembrance of the previous day's events hit her. Oh, God, she had behaved so stupidly. And that after the embarrassment she'd suffered at Maria Sholti's hands.

Pushing herself up into a sitting position, Tess rested her elbows on her knees and pushed frustrated hands into her hair. The whole outing had been a mistake, from start to finish. Castelli should never have taken her with him, and, just because he had, she shouldn't have run away with the idea that he was attracted to her.

How had that happened? All right, he'd given her some pretty smouldering looks, but he was an Italian, for God's sake. Italians were supposed to be the most romantic race in the world, weren't they? She'd obviously read more into it than he could possibly have meant. She should have been on her guard. After that scene at the Sholtis' hotel, she should have been wary of any uncharacteristic behaviour on his part. A man who could treat his daughter so coldly was surely not to be trusted.

Yet what had happened on the beach hadn't been entirely her fault, she consoled herself. She'd provoked him, yes, and he'd responded. It had been as simple—and as complicated—as that. She should have let him take his walk alone.

90

She should never have tagged along. If she'd stayed and finished her salad she wouldn't be berating herself now.

And she wouldn't be facing the ignominy of further humiliation when she saw him again.

If she saw him again, she amended, though she really had little expectation that she wouldn't. Ashley was still missing; Marco was still missing. And until that particular problem was solved, she was going to have to live with it. And with him.

She threw back the sheet and slid her legs off the bed. Sitting here brooding about it wasn't going to achieve anything. The gallery wouldn't open itself, and, despite her anger with Ashley, she had promised to look after the place in her absence.

All the same, as she stood in the shower she couldn't help reliving the agony of the ride home. Although Castelli had attempted to restore their earlier camaraderie, he had been fighting a losing battle where she was concerned. Her own responses had been monosyllabic, she remembered, cringing at the way she'd blocked his every overture. She'd let him see exactly how hurt she'd been, and he must have been so relieved when they'd reached San Michele and he'd been able to drop her at the gallery. She'd probably convinced him she was no better than Ashley, after all. He no doubt considered he had had a lucky escape.

With thoughts like these for company, Tess didn't spend long in the shower. Towelling herself dry, she contented herself with running a comb through her hair before dressing in a lemon chemise top and a green and blue Indian cotton skirt. Canvas boots completed her outfit and, after viewing herself without enthusiasm in the mirror of the carved armoire where Ashley kept her clothes, Tess left the apartment.

The morning passed, thankfully without incident. The only visitor she had who wasn't a would-be customer was Silvio and he seemed to find nothing amiss with her appearance.

'*Cara,*' he exclaimed, his use of the familiar endearment reminding her painfully of Castelli, 'how are you today? You are feeling better, *spero*?'

'Better?' Tess frowned. 'I'm afraid I don't understand.'

'*Mas, ieri,*' said Silvio, wide eyed. 'Yesterday. You close the gallery early, *no*? *Naturalmente*, I think you are not well.'

'Oh.' Tess felt her face heat. 'Um—yes. I did close early. You're right. But—' she couldn't tell an outright lie '—it wasn't because I was ill.'

'No?' Silvio gave her an inquiring look and she knew she had to elaborate.

'No.' She paused. 'I—it was such a lovely day, I decided to—to take a little time off.'

'Ah.' Silvio regarded her with narrowed eyes. 'And you enjoyed this—this time off?'

No.

'Very much,' she said, deciding one white lie was in order. And then, to distract him, 'Isn't it hot today? I've got the fan going but it just seems to be moving the air around.'

'It is warm air,' he pointed out drily, and she wondered if he was entirely satisfied with her reply. 'So, do you have any plans for lunch?'

'Lunch?' Tess had the feeling she would never want to eat lunch again. 'Oh—no.' Then, realising what was coming next, 'I'm too busy to think about lunch. Taking time off is all very well, but it just means the work piles up in your absence.'

Silvio glanced about him at the empty gallery. 'It does not seem so busy to me.'

'Oh, it's paperwork,' said Tess, realising she was having to lie again. 'Honestly, you'd be surprised at the number of enquiries Ashley gets about this or that artist. And then there are the bills…'

'In other words you do not wish to have lunch with me,' remarked Silvio flatly. 'You do not have to—if you will forgive the pun—draw me a picture, Tess. It is obvious some other man has—what do you say?—beaten me to it, *no*? Who is he, eh? Do I know him?'

'No!' Tess spoke impulsively and then, realising her words could easily be misconstrued, she hastily amended her answer. 'That is, there is no other man, Silvio. Um— not here, anyway,' she added, her face burning with embarrassment. 'I just can't keep taking time off, that's all. It wouldn't be fair to—to Signor Scottolino.'

Silvio shrugged. 'As you say.'

'I'm sorry.'

'*Sì. Anch'io, cara.*' Me, too. He gave her a small, strangely knowing smile. 'Do not work too hard, *ragazza*. All work and no play is not good, *no*? *Ciao!*'

Tess breathed a sigh of relief as he disappeared through the open doorway and, deciding she'd earned a strong cup of black coffee, she went to put water into the pot. But she couldn't help wondering if Silvio's visit had been as innocent as he'd pretended. Could he possibly have seen her leaving with Castelli the day before?

Of course he could, but if he had there was nothing she could do about it now. And, besides, she had a perfectly legitimate excuse for the outing if she was asked. But she wouldn't be. Silvio had said his piece and no one else was interested. Except Maria and her husband, she amended. And they knew nothing about what had happened after she and Castelli had left the *albergo*.

Thank goodness!

By midday Tess was feeling a little more relaxed. Her fears that Castelli might decide to pay her another unexpected visit had not been realised, and, with her stomach reminding her that she'd not had any breakfast that morning, she decided to slip out to the bakery to buy a sandwich for her lunch.

She'd only closed the gallery for a few minutes. The bakery wasn't far. But when she came hurrying back along the parade of shops she saw a woman trying the door with obvious impatience. With the blinds pulled up, it appeared that the gallery was open, and Tess thought it was just her luck that a customer had arrived in the short time she'd been away.

'*Mi scusi,*' she called, reaching the woman just as she was turning away. The woman turned back and Tess saw she was older than she'd thought. '*Eccomi, signora. Posso aiutare?*' Can I help you?

Dark brows arched aristocratically over equally dark eyes. The woman was tall and exquisitely dressed in a taupe silk suit and high heels. Because of her height, she towered over Tess, her whole manner one of undisguised condescension.

Yet for all that, there was something familiar about her. Tess knew she'd never seen the woman before but the annoying sense of familiarity remained. Tess had barely registered the fact that she reminded her of Maria Castelli when the woman spoke, and her words gave substance to the thought.

'Miss Daniels, *e*?' she inquired coldly, looking down her long nose at Tess in a manner intended to intimidate. 'Ah, *sì.* You recognise the name. Let us go inside, Miss Daniels. I desire to speak to you.'

'All right.' Tess was too taken aback by this turn of events to offer any resistance and she unlocked the door and allowed the older woman to precede her into the gallery. Then, gathering herself, she said, a little less submissively, 'Do we know one another, *signora*?'

The woman didn't immediately proffer a reply. Instead, she stood in the centre of the floor surveying the paintings that lined the walls with evident dislike. They were not all good paintings, Tess acknowledged, but some of them weren't at all bad. They didn't deserve the contempt with which they were being regarded. Her visitor was acting as if they were little better than trash.

Or perhaps she'd got it wrong, she mused suddenly. Perhaps it was she whom the woman considered to be trash. That would fit if she was some relation of Maria Castelli—or rather Maria *Sholti*. And despite the relief she'd felt at

Castelli's non-appearance, now she felt a growing sense of resentment that he should have sent this woman in his place.

The woman swung round at last. 'I know *of* you, Miss Daniels,' she said, and Tess had to remind herself of what she'd asked moments before. 'My son has spoken of you to me. I am Lucia di Castelli.' She said the name arrogantly. 'The boy your sister has corrupted is my grandson.'

Tess caught her breath. So this was Castelli's mother. She should have guessed. The similarity wasn't totally confined to his daughter.

But Castelli wasn't going to help her now and, holding up her head, she said stiffly, 'We don't know that Ashley has done anything of the kind.'

'Oh, I think we do, *signorina*.' Lucia was scornful. 'I cannot think of any other reason why a woman approaching thirty should encourage the attentions of an impressionable child, can you?'

'Marco's hardly a child,' protested Tess indignantly. 'In England, boys of sixteen can be quite—mature.'

'And there you have it, Miss Daniels.' Lucia's lips curled. 'As you say, in England things are very different indeed. Young single women think nothing of having a child—children—with several different partners. Marriage is considered an outdated institution and the church's teachings are ignored. That is not how things are done in Italy, Miss Daniels. Here we respect our institutions, we respect our elders. And we expect visitors to our country to do the same.'

Tess licked her dry lips. 'You paint a very unattractive picture of my country, *signora*,' she said, keeping her voice calm with a definite effort. 'But I can assure you that we are not a totally godless society. As with everything, the truth lies somewhere in between.'

Lucia snorted. 'You would say that, *naturalmente*.'

'Yes, I would.' Tess gained a little confidence from the fact that the woman didn't immediately contradict her. 'We are not heathens, *signora*. And how honest is it for a woman to marry one man and have an affair with another? Is that considered acceptable in Italy?'

A faint trace of colour entered Lucia's cheeks at her words. 'You have been speaking to Rafe, have you not?' she demanded harshly, shocking Tess by the vehemence of her tone. 'Of course you have. That is why he is so—so *sensibile* to your feelings. He sees in you a justification for his own actions.'

'No!' Tess was horrified. She'd spoken impulsively, never thinking that Castelli's mother might associate her words with her son's divorce. 'I mean, yes, I've spoken to your son, *signora*. You know that. He thought I might know where Ashley was.'

'But you do not?'

'No.' Tess was polite, but firm.

'Did my son tell you that he has spoken with his daughter, also?' Lucia continued. 'Maria is married and lives in Viali, some distance from here.'

The query seemed innocent enough at face value, but Tess was wary. Was it possible that Lucia di Castelli knew she had accompanied her son the day before? Had he told her? Had Maria? And if not, how was she supposed to answer that?

'He—I—yes, I knew,' she mumbled at last, unwilling to venture further. Besides, why shouldn't Castelli have mentioned that she'd gone to Viali with him? With certain abstentions in his narrative, of course.

She took a deep breath and then was relieved when a young couple came into the gallery. They were obviously holiday-makers and she doubted they intended to buy anything. But her visitor didn't know that.

'Was there a reason for your visit, *signora*?' she asked, indicating the newcomers. 'Because if not, I have customers. If you hoped I might have any more information than I've given your son, then I'm afraid I must disappoint you.'

Lucia's lips tightened. 'I think you know more than you

Play The

Lucky Hearts Game

and get...

FREE BOOKS & a FREE GIFT...
YOURS to KEEP!

Yes! I have scratched off the silver card.
Please send me my **FREE BOOKS** and
FREE MYSTERY GIFT. I understand
that I am under no obligation to purchase any
books as explained on the back of this card.
I am over 18 years of age.

Scratch Here!
then look below to see
what you can claim...

P4GI

Mrs/Miss/Ms/Mr	Initials

BLOCK CAPITALS PLEASE

Surname _____

Address _____

_____

Postcode _____

Twenty-one gets you
4 FREE BOOKS and a
MYSTERY GIFT!

Twenty gets you
1 FREE BOOK and a
MYSTERY GIFT!

Nineteen gets you
1 FREE BOOK!

TRY AGAIN!

NO STAMP NEEDED!

THE READER SERVICE™
FREE BOOK OFFER
FREEPOST CN81
CROYDON
CR9 3WZ

NO STAMP
NECESSARY
IF POSTED IN
THE U.K. OR N.I.

are saying, Miss Daniels. Unlike my son, I am not beguiled by a sympathetic manner and a pretty face!'

Tess was taken aback by her rudeness and she glanced awkwardly about her wondering if their exchange could be heard by anyone else. But to her relief the young couple had moved to the farthest side of the gallery and she thought it was unlikely that they'd noticed anything amiss.

'I think you'd better go, *signora*,' she said in a low voice, refusing to humour her any longer. 'I'm working and I'm sure you have better things to do than stand here wasting my time. I'm sorry about your grandson, I really am. But there's nothing I can do about it. Ashley didn't confide in me before she took off.'

Lucia's nostrils flared, and for a moment Tess expected another rebuke. But then, amazingly, the woman's haughty arrogance crumbled, and with a gesture of defeat she pulled a handkerchief out of her purse.

Tess didn't know which was worse, having Castelli's mother berating her as an accomplice or breaking down in front of her. Tears were streaming down the woman's face now and she was obviously distressed. Any moment Tess's customers were going to notice and, despite herself, she couldn't allow that to happen.

With a feeling of resignation, she took Lucia by the arm and led her back into the office. Then, after seating her at Ashley's desk, she indicated the small bathroom. 'You can rest here,' she said. 'Come out when you're feeling better. No one will disturb you. I'll see to that.'

As she'd suspected, the young couple had no intention of buying anything, and she had to acknowledge that Signor Scottolino had a point. Since she'd been looking after the gallery, she'd sold a grand total of three paintings, which was clearly not enough profit to pay the bills.

It was another fifteen minutes before she remembered her sandwich. She'd put it down as she was talking to Signora di Castelli and now she saw it wilting in the noonday heat. She would have liked to have gone into the office and made herself some fresh coffee. Signora di Castelli might even like one. Although, remembering her son's reaction when he'd tried the filtered brew, she couldn't guarantee it.

However, she'd told the woman she wouldn't be disturbed and she kept her promises. It was obviously going to take a little time for Lucia to compose herself again. Until then, Tess contented herself with straightening the pictures, picking up a leaf that had blown through the open doorway, and adjusting the blinds to limit the sunlight.

After half an hour had gone by, however, she was beginning to get anxious. All sorts of thoughts ran through her head, not least the worry that Lucia might do something desperate in her grief. Which was silly, she knew. The situation was not that serious. They might not know exactly where Marco was, but if he was with Ashley, he could hardly come to any harm.

Or could he? Tess supposed it depended what your interpretation of harm was. As far as Lucia was concerned, Ashley was little better than a baby-snatcher. The fact that Marco sounded like a precocious teenager seemed to mean nothing to her.

At the end of forty-five minutes, Tess was desperate. All right, she'd promised not to disturb the woman, but that was ages ago now. Squaring her shoulders, she picked up her sandwich and went to the half-open door of the office. 'Signora di Castelli,' she said, pushing it wider. 'Are you feeling better?'

She needn't have bothered with the softly-softly approach. The office was empty. While she'd been fretting in the gallery, Lucia must have let herself out of the back exit. So much for Tess worrying about her. She had evidently dried her eyes and made herself scarce.

Tess didn't know whether she felt relieved or resentful. She was glad the woman had gone, of course, but she might have asked her permission to use the back door. As it was, it was standing ajar and Tess went to close it. It would have been all the same if she'd had valuable paintings on the premises. With the alarm turned off, a thief could have had a field-day.

A check of her bag assured her that there'd been no intruders in her absence. Her passport was still there and the several hundred Euros she'd brought for the trip. She frowned suddenly. She could have sworn her passport had been in the side pocket of her backpack as it had been when Castelli had asked to see it. But now it resided in the main compartment alongside her wallet-purse.

She shrugged. She must have made a mistake when she'd put it away. She hadn't needed it for the last couple of days so she couldn't be absolutely sure which compartment she'd put it in. Castelli had got her so flustered, she might have put it anywhere. In any case, so long as she had it, that was the important thing.

She spent a couple of minutes emptying the coffee-pot and refilling the reservoir. Then, after putting several spoonfuls of ready-ground coffee into the filter, she sat down at the desk to have her sandwich.

It wasn't very appetising. Having waited for almost an hour, it was definitely dry. Thankfully it was cheese. She was afraid any meat would have proved inedible. Even so, if she hadn't been so hungry, she might have put it into the bin.

As she drank her coffee she idly opened the drawers of the desk. She was not really looking for anything, but she was still conscious of the doubts she'd had before. Once again, she was fairly sure nothing was missing, and as she'd riffled through the drawers herself days ago, looking for any clues to Ashley's whereabouts, she wasn't really surprised when she found nothing useful now.

The niggling doubts remained, though, and she wondered if Lucia di Castelli had searched the office before she'd left. It would explain the discrepancy about her passport. And perhaps explain the reason why she'd left without saying goodbye. Though, remembering Castelli's mother, Tess doubted whether she'd care if she offended her. Until her emotions had got the better of her, she'd been doing a fairly good job of making Tess feel she was equally to blame.

It was a long afternoon. She had a couple more customers, one of whom actually bought a painting of the pretty resort of Portofino further up the coast. The other was a young Frenchman, who was evidently on holiday. His main interest was in flirting with Tess, and she guessed Ashley had enjoyed this aspect of her job.

But she didn't. She was in no mood to be flattered and she became impatient when he refused to go. She eventually resorted to blackmail, picking up the phone and threatening to call *la polizia*. She wouldn't have, of course, but thankfully her ploy was successful.

She closed the gallery early, not wanting to risk Silvio coming round to offer her dinner. She couldn't help thinking she'd never been so popular in her life. Of course, at home her work kept her busy and the men with whom she worked were not her type. Those that weren't married were often too boyish. Her friend, Maggie, always said they were like overgrown school kids themselves.

Tess had only had one real relationship and that had been with a boy she'd met at college. They'd kept in touch for a couple of years afterwards, but Tess's moving to Derbyshire had put paid to their affair. He'd eventually written that he'd found someone else, and Tess remembered she had been more relieved than sorry. Maybe she just wasn't cut out to find a partner, she thought as she drove back to Ashley's apartment. The quintessential schoolmistress, that was her.

An image of herself and Castelli on the beach flashed into her mind, but she quickly pushed it away. Apart from the fact that she'd initiated that encounter, it was obvious he'd only been humouring her. He was a virile man and perhaps he'd been flattered at a younger woman coming on to him. Even if he'd felt sorry for her, and that was not an alternative she wanted to consider, it hadn't been hard for him to fake a convincing response.

He'd certainly convinced her, she thought bitterly. Her

stomach still quivered at the memory of the feelings he had aroused inside her. She could still taste his kiss, still feel the heat of his tongue in her mouth. She knew he'd been physically aroused. That was something he hadn't been able to hide. Yet even so, he'd found it easy to pull away.

And that hurt. She couldn't understand how he'd been able to turn off his emotions like a switch. Or perhaps his emotions hadn't been involved. She'd obviously been wrong to think he'd been as eager as she had. While she'd been anticipating how exciting making love with him would be, he'd had an entirely different agenda.

But what agenda? If he hadn't avoided the subject of Ashley all the way back to San Michele, she'd have suspected that finding her sister had still been his principal concern. He could have thought that seducing her might produce some hitherto unspoken confession. That she'd be so bemused by his lovemaking, she'd betray any confidence she'd been given.

But she'd been wrong about that, too. While she'd been aching with longings now suppressed, Castelli had spoken of his interest in wine, and the grape harvest, and how lots of people were leaving the towns to start a new life in the country. He'd behaved as if nothing untoward had happened, as if he was totally unaware of how she was feeling.

She was sure she'd never forgive him for that. Being rejected was one thing; being ignored was something else. But, with Ashley's example to follow, what had she expected? Castelli didn't want anything more from her than information. He didn't care about her. He only cared about his son.

CHAPTER NINE

TESS bought some chicken and vegetables on her way home and stir-fried them for her supper. She wasn't particularly hungry, but there was no point in starving because she'd made a fool of herself over a man. She wasn't the first woman to do that and she wouldn't be the last. And she at least had the satisfaction of knowing that Castelli hadn't been totally indifferent to her.

She'd bought some wine, too, but, although she left it on the counter, she didn't open the bottle. It was one thing making herself a decent meal for once. Drinking a whole bottle of Lambrusco on her own was something else. Instead, after making a gallant effort to enjoy the food, she made herself a cup of instant coffee and carried it out onto the balcony adjoining the bedroom to drink.

It was almost dark and already a string of lights had sprung up along the waterfront. She could smell the aromas of food cooking, of garlic and other herbs, and hear the sound of voices from the street below. Somewhere a saxophone was playing a haunting melody, bringing the unwilling brush of tears to her eyes. This should have been such a simple visit, she thought miserably. When had it all started to go wrong?

She knew the answer, of course. It had been wrong from the beginning. Andrea wasn't ill; Ashley hadn't been called home to look after her. Instead, she'd taken off with a boy who was far too young for her, causing embarrassment to her sister and distress to his family.

Tess caught her breath as another thought struck her. It was Friday tomorrow, and, remembering what Ashley's mother had said, she was surprised she hadn't heard from her again. She prayed it wasn't because Andrea had decided to make good on her threat and come to Italy herself.

Oh, God, that was all she needed, for her stepmother to show up unannounced. Where would she stay? The apartment wasn't really big enough for two people and Tess could well imagine that she'd be the one expected to find alternative accommodation.

A burst of laughter from the courtyard below was reassuring. Obviously some of her neighbours were having a party and she envied them their careless enjoyment. She thought if she'd lived here, like Ashley, she'd have made an effort to make friends with the other tenants. She'd noticed a couple of younger people going in and out of the building and they'd looked friendly enough. It would have been fun to brush up on her Italian, too. Fun, also, to invite someone in to share her supper. Someone who, unlike Silvio, would not expect anything more than good food and casual conversation.

She was considering opening the wine, after all, as a compensation for standing here all alone, when everyone else seemed to be having such a good time, when there was a knock on her door.

Tess froze for a moment and then took a swift look at her watch. It was after nine o'clock. Far too late for a casual caller. It had to be Andrea, she thought in dismay. Who else could it be?

She was tempted to pretend she wasn't in. Ashley's mother didn't have a key, obviously, and she doubted the old caretaker would let a complete stranger into the apartment. But she would have to face her sooner or later and she didn't have the heart to send her away. Depositing her empty coffee-cup in the sink, she composed herself and went to open the door.

It wasn't Andrea. The man standing outside was probably the person she'd least expected to see, and she stared at him in total disbelief.

'You should have checked who your caller was before

you opened the door,' Castelli said roughly, by way of a greeting. 'Who were you expecting?'

'No one.' Tess was too shocked to lie to him. 'I wasn't *expecting* anyone.' Then, in an attempt to regain the initiative, she added defiantly, 'What are you doing here, *signore?* Slumming?'

Castelli's mouth compressed. 'I will not dignify that remark with a response,' he declared harshly. Then, with a glance beyond her into the apartment, 'Are you alone?'

Tess caught her breath. 'What's that to you?' she retorted, in no mood to respect his feelings. The image of his regretful—no, pitying—expression when he'd pushed her away from him on the beach was still painfully acute. How dared he come here and behave as if he had any right to question her behaviour? Unless this visit was to get her to apologise for what she'd said to his mother. If it was, he was wasting his time.

He sighed now. 'May I come in?'

'Why?'

'Because I wish to speak with you,' he said patiently. 'And I would prefer it if we could speak privately.'

Tess felt mutinous. 'I don't think I want to speak to you tonight, *signore*,' she said, squashing the little spark of hope that he might have come to apologise himself. Besides which, it was better if she didn't spend any time alone with him. Crazy as it was, she didn't trust herself where he was concerned. She waited a beat and then added defensively, 'I was just going to bed.'

His expression was sceptical. 'At nine-fifteen? I do not think so, *cara*.'

'Don't call me that.' Tess was angry. 'And it's really none of your business what I do, *signore*. I'll be at the gallery in the morning. If you have anything to say to me, perhaps you could save it until then?'

'Tess!'

His use of her name was almost her undoing. His voice had softened, deepened to a dark, persuasive drawl. It caused a quiver in her stomach, an aching need that spread to every part of her body. Despite herself, emotions stirred inside her, and she had to lift a hand to the frame of the door to support her shaking legs.

But somehow, she found the words to say, 'If this is your way of getting me to apologise for what I said to your mother, you're going to be unlucky.' She straightened her spine. 'I meant what I said, and you can tell her from me that I don't think much of the way she left without even closing the door behind her.'

Castelli's brows drew together. Then, before she realised what he intended to do, he swept her hand aside and stepped across the threshold. She was forced to move out of his way to avoid coming into contact with his hard body and he used the opportunity it gave him to slam the door.

The sound reverberated round the apartment and she was gearing herself to demand that he get out of there, at once, when he said, 'What the hell are you talking about? I did not even know you had met my mother.'

Tess's lips parted. She didn't want to believe him but there was something so convincing in his gaze that she couldn't help herself. 'I—she came to the gallery,' she said stiffly. She lifted her shoulders. 'I thought you knew.'

'Well, obviously, I did not.'

'No.' Tess conceded the point. 'I'm sorry. I naturally assumed that was why you were here.'

Castelli made a strangely defeated gesture. 'Naturally,' he said flatly, walking across the living room to stand staring down at the lights of the harbour below. 'What other reason could there be?'

Tess caught her lower lip between her teeth. She would not feel sorry for him, she thought. That way lay danger. And, as she didn't have a satisfactory answer for him, she indulged herself for a moment by pretending he really had come here to see her.

With his back to her, she was able to look at him unobserved and her eyes lingered on broad shoulders, shown to advantage in a close-fitting black polo shirt. His black draw-string trousers were tight over his buttocks but only hinted at the powerful muscles of his legs. Taken as a whole, his outfit didn't look like something he would wear to a social gathering. Which meant what? That he had come here to see her, after all?

The breath she was about to take caught in her throat and all her bones seemed to melt beneath her. A purely visceral surge of longing gripped her, but before she could say something foolish, comprehension dawned.

'Ashley,' she said quickly before her panicked breathing could betray her. 'You're here about Ashley.' She paused to take another calming gulp of air. 'Have you found out where they are?'

He turned then, pushing his hands into the pockets of his pants as he did so, tautening the soft cotton across his thighs. In spite of herself, Tess's eyes were drawn there. She dragged them away again as he said, 'No,' in a flat, expressionless voice. Then, as if he too was finding it hard to speak casually, he continued, 'Verdicci has had no luck in Genova. If your sister has hired a car, she has hired it under another name.'

'Oh.' Tess swallowed. 'Could she do that?'

'If she had an accomplice,' replied Castelli carelessly. 'Do you know if she has any friends here in San Michele?'

Tess shook her head. 'Not as far as I know,' she replied, sure that Ashley had never mentioned any particular friend to her. Certainly no one who might be willing to assist her in doing something that sounded vaguely illegal. 'She's only lived here for nine months. Hardly long enough to get that close to anyone.'

'Except Marco,' Castelli observed softly, and Tess felt his frustration. Then, his eyes intent, 'Tell me about my mother. I assume she came to ask you about your sister. What did she say to upset you?'

Tess shrugged. 'Why do you think she upset me?' she

argued defensively, and a faint smile tugged at his lean, attractive mouth.

'You said that if I had come for an apology, I would be unlucky, *no*?' he responded drily. 'Please, humour me. I would like to know her reasons for speaking with you.'

Tess sighed. 'Oh—you know. She thought I might know more than I'd said.'

'That you might know more than you had told me?' he suggested shrewdly, and she nodded.

'Something like that.'

'Mmm.' He withdrew his hands from his pockets and crossed them over his chest, tucking his fingers beneath his arms. 'I guess she was unhappy with the results I had achieved. Did she tell you what a disappointment I had been to her as both a husband and a father?'

'No!' Tess was shocked. 'She didn't say anything like that.'

'But she did imply that I was to blame for allowing Marco to become involved with your sister?'

'No.' Tess shook her head. 'It was Ashley she vilified, not you. Or Marco. She said that Ashley had corrupted her grandson. That he was just a child. And when I said that boys of sixteen were not considered children in England, she criticised that, as well.' She paused. 'You—you were hardly mentioned.'

Castelli was sardonic. 'You disappoint me.'

'Well, I'm sure she didn't approve of you associating with me,' Tess appended swiftly. She pressed her hands together at her midriff, aware that she'd changed into an old pair of denim cut-offs when she'd got home from the gallery and they were hardly flattering. 'She probably thinks that I'll corrupt you, too.'

Castelli regarded her with mild amusement. 'Do you think that is possible, *cara*? I am not an impressionable boy to be dazzled by a woman's looks. In my experience, a pretty face has a limited appeal. If I had to choose, I would pick brains over beauty every time.'

'How noble of you.' Tess couldn't hide her bitterness. 'Is that why your wife left you? Because she couldn't live up to such high ideals?'

It was an unforgivable thing to say, but Tess refused to feel any remorse. She resented the fact that he'd come here, that he'd felt he had the right to force his way into the apartment on some pretext she had yet to discover. All right, the way she'd behaved on the beach had probably given him the notion that she'd be willing to do just about anything he asked of her. But that had been a moment of madness that she had no intention of repeating. Ever.

Castelli moved then and she had to steel herself not to put the bar that divided the kitchenette from the rest of the room between them. But all he did was rub his palms over his spread thighs. He seemed to be more thoughtful than angry. It was as if he was considering her words and deciding how to answer her. Perhaps she'd been a little too close for comfort, she thought eagerly, feeling a momentary surge of revenge.

When he said, 'I do not wish to discuss my wife with you,' she felt almost euphoric. And when he continued, 'Her reasons for leaving me are not part of this equation,' she was sure she had bloodied a nerve.

'So I was right,' she said, amazed at her own temerity. 'You're just like your mother and Maria. You Castellis think you're never wrong!'

'No!' The word was harsh and angry and for the first time Tess was aware that they were alone. 'You are not right,' he said, coming towards her. 'Gina and I did not separate because of any high ideals on my part. Not unless you consider the fact that she preferred to sleep in other beds than mine no justification.'

Tess did retreat behind the bar then.

She felt mortified and ashamed. She'd been so intent on scoring points, she hadn't considered the wounds she might have been inflicting.

'I'm sorry,' she said unhappily. 'I shouldn't have said

that.' She spread her hands along the bar, nails digging into the plastic rim. She licked her lips and when he didn't speak she added, with a weak attempt at humour, 'Blame your mother. I got used to defending myself with her.'

Castelli's lips tightened. 'You do it very well,' he said, facing her across the narrow divide. 'But you are wrong about me. My opinion of my own character is very poor.'

'Is it?'

Tess couldn't prevent the rejoinder and, because it seemed as if she couldn't speak to him without being provoking, she picked up the bottle of wine she'd left on the counter earlier. The label meant nothing to her but she pretended to examine it anyway. Anything to avoid looking at him, from responding to that dangerous sexuality that he wore as naturally as his skin.

'It seems you had the last word. As far as my mother was concerned,' he said after a moment, and she wondered if he was trying to defuse the situation, too. It made it even harder to remember why she'd been so angry with him. But at least talking about his mother seemed harmless enough.

'It was only because she got upset,' she admitted now, putting down the bottle and opening a drawer. Rummaging around for the corkscrew gave her another excuse not to look at him. 'I suggested she went into the office to compose herself. Then she let herself out the back without even closing the door behind her.'

Castelli snorted. '*She* got upset,' he echoed disbelievingly. 'That does not sound like the woman I know. *Cara*, Lucia does not get upset. Not unless it is for some purpose of her own.'

'Well, perhaps she wanted to spend some time alone in the office,' offered Tess, finding the corkscrew and pulling a rueful face. 'I—well, I'm not absolutely sure about this, but I think she might have searched Ashley's desk.'

'*Non credo!*' Castelli was shocked, she could tell. 'No. Lucia may be many things, *cara*, but she is not a thief!'

'I believe you.' Tess sighed. 'But I think she was looking for something all the same.'

'Cosa?' What?

Tess shrugged, and then, because she'd succeeded in finding the corkscrew, she felt obliged to use it. She was fitting the screw into the cork when Castelli came round the bar and took the implement from her. 'Let me do that,' he said, with obvious impatience. 'Then perhaps you will explain what you are talking about.'

Tess didn't argue with him. Stepping back, she let him have his way. But the kitchenette was tiny and he was now much too close for comfort. She couldn't get past him. Not without rubbing up against him. And that was the last thing she wanted to do in her present state of emotional upheaval.

Instead, she kept her gaze riveted on his hands in an effort to distract herself. But she was uncomfortably aware of the strength in his chest and arms, the way his tight shirt outlined the taut muscles of his stomach.

He was all male, all man, and she wouldn't have been human if she hadn't responded to it. Particularly after what had happened between them before. Her breasts puckered in anticipation of a caress they were not going to receive, and she crossed her arms across her body in an effort to hide her reaction from him.

Her mouth was dry and, realising he was waiting for an explanation, she said quickly, 'I think your mother was looking for information about Ashley. Perhaps she thought I'd missed something when I looked through the desk myself.'

Castelli pulled out the cork before replying. Then, setting the bottle down on the counter, he said, 'So did she find anything?'

'Not as far as I know.' Tess was wary. 'Why? Do you think she did?'

Castelli made a dismissive gesture. 'Until this moment, I did not even know she had visited the gallery,' he said drily. He frowned. 'But I have not seen her today, so who knows?'

Tess's lips parted. 'I hope you don't still think I've been keeping Ashley's whereabouts a secret from you,' she exclaimed indignantly, and Castelli gave her a speaking look. 'You needn't deny it,' she continued hotly. 'That's why you've come here, isn't it? Because your mother's disappeared and you think I might know where she's gone?'

'Do not be so ridiculous,' he told her impatiently. 'I have just told you, I did not even know Lucia had been to the gallery when I came here.'

'So you said.'

'What is that supposed to mean?'

'Well, I only have your word that you didn't know about her visit,' said Tess challengingly. 'And you must admit, you haven't given me a good reason for coming here yet.'

Castelli leaned back against the counter, resting his hands on the worn plastic at either side of him. Then, with gentle irony, he said, 'Well, obviously I am not here at your invitation. Let us be honest with one another. Do you want me to go?'

Yes!

But she couldn't say it. Didn't want to say it, if she was completely truthful with herself.

'I'm sure you know exactly what I want,' she said at last, turning away to open the cupboard door above her. But as he'd opened the wine, it would be churlish not to offer him a glass. 'I think there are some glasses in here somewhere. Why don't you have some wine before you go?'

'Do I have a choice?'

She started, almost dropping the two glasses she'd found in the cupboard. The words had been spoken immediately behind her, his warm breath fanning the damp curls that nestled at her nape.

Looking down, she saw he had placed a hand on the unit at either side of her now and she was successfully trapped within the barrier of his arms. If she turned around, her face would only be inches from his. Goodness knew if there'd be room enough to take a breath and she didn't feel confident enough to try.

'What are you doing?' she asked instead, amazed her voice sounded almost normal. 'Do you want some wine or don't you?'

'If it is anything like your coffee, perhaps I will pass,' he chided lightly. And then, with sudden passion, '*Dio*, Tess, are you ever going to forgive me for what happened yesterday? I know I hurt you. Do not bother to deny it. And I want you to know I have suffered for it ever since.'

CHAPTER TEN

SHE didn't believe him.

'You flatter yourself,' Tess said now, taking a shaky breath. She despised the feelings of weakness his lying words evoked. 'I've forgotten all about it.'

'I do not think so.' He was inflexible. 'If you had forgotten all about it, *cara*, you would not be standing here, afraid to turn and face me.' He paused, blowing on her neck. '*Non abbia paura.* Do not be afraid of me, *cara*. I will do nothing you do not want me to do.'

Tess felt a momentary twinge of cynicism. He could say that because he thought he knew what she was thinking, what she was feeling. And perhaps he did, but he would never know it. She had no intention of letting him make a fool of her again.

Steeling herself against his flagrant magnetism, she put the glass down and forced herself to turn then. But she pressed her hips against the unit behind her, taking shallow little breaths to avoid the inevitable brush of her breasts against his chest. Fixing her gaze on some point beyond his right ear, she said stiffly, 'And if I want you to go?'

His sigh was heartfelt. 'Then I will do as you wish,' he said heavily, his hands falling to his sides. 'But before I do, there is something I have to say to you.'

'What?' Tess was uneasy, not least because she was still trapped by his powerful frame.

'You asked why I had come here,' he answered her softly. 'Will you believe me if I say that my only reason for doing so was because I wanted to see you again?'

'No!' The word burst from her lips and this time she had no compunction about pushing him aside and escaping across the room. She should have known better, she thought. He would use any means to get his own way and she was making it easy for him. It seemed tonight that he'd decided to take her up on her oh-so-unsubtle advances and she'd almost given in. 'I think you'd better go, *signore*. Before I call the *custode* and have you thrown out!'

Which was ridiculous considering the old caretaker was seventy if he was a day.

He shook his head now. 'I do not think you will do that, *cara*,' he said flatly. 'You would not wish to make a scene.'

'Don't bet on it.' Tess hated it that he could read her so easily. 'I know you think that because Ashley appears not to have any scruples, I'm the same. But I'm not. What happened on the beach was a mistake. It was sensible to stop it as you did.'

He sighed. 'You may be right,' he said wearily, raking a resigned hand through his hair. 'And it was probably a mistake to come here. Put it down to a moment of weakness. I wanted to see you and I did not stop to think how it might look to you.'

'Oh, please.' Tess had heard enough. 'We both know why you came here and it wasn't to beg my forgiveness or anything as high-minded as that. You were at a loose end and you remembered how easy I'd been to seduce. I can't exactly blame you for that but I don't have to prove it.'

Castelli gave a harsh exclamation. 'You are so wrong,' he said vehemently. 'Wrong about the reasons I came here and wrong about what happened on the beach.'

'I don't think so,' she began, but her words were overridden by his.

'What?' he demanded bitterly. 'Do you think if I was the kind of man you seem to think I am, I would have been so *galante*? And by the way, I did not seduce you, *cara*. I wanted to. Ah, *sì*, I admit I wanted to. Why not? You are a very desirable woman. But, contrary to your beliefs, I do not make love with women who are only a few years older than my own daughter. I have standards, too, and I know I am too old for you.' He shrugged. 'That is all I wanted to tell you.'

Tess stared at him. 'So why come here? Why make a special journey just to tell me something I don't believe and which I don't think you believe either.'

Castelli's lips twisted. 'You are a hard woman, Tess,' he said heavily. 'And perhaps you are right. Perhaps I did come here hoping you might be glad to see me. I like you. I like being with you. And if you think I wanted to let you go the other afternoon…' He sighed. '*Dio*, I do not think even you can be that insensitive.'

Tess felt the force of his words deep in the pit of her stomach. Her body hummed with the sexual energy he was generating and, although she was trying so very hard to remain unmoved by his appeal, there was something disturbingly vulnerable in his face.

'So—so what are you saying?' she asked, despising herself for giving him an opening. 'That the only reason you let me go was because you believe you're too old for me?'

'Not entirely.' His response flattened a momentary spurt of excitement. 'I was thinking of myself, too.'

'Why am I not surprised?' Tess shook her head. And then caught her breath when he strode forward and grabbed her wrist.

'*Stammi a sentire!*' he commanded harshly. 'Listen to me!' His thumb pressed hard on the fine veins on the inner side of her wrist. 'You think you are the only one with something to lose here, but you are wrong. And I am not willing to provide a romantic diversion for someone who is only looking for a holiday affair.'

Tess swallowed. 'I—I see.'

'Do you?' He was sardonic. 'And do you also see that touching you like this is a mistake?'

Tess quivered. 'Then let me go.'

'To do what?' He arched his dark brows, his eyes insistent, disturbing, intent. 'Leave you with the impression that I am not strong enough to control my own feelings? *Dio*,

Tess, this was not meant to happen. You are my connection to my son. That was supposed to be the only reason why we spent any time together.'

'And it was,' said Tess breathlessly, intensely aware of the sinuous yet immensely strong hold he had on her wrist. The heat from his fingers enveloped her arm, spread unchecked into her shoulder. She licked her dry lips, hardly aware of what she was doing. Then, persuasively, 'Why don't we have a glass of wine? I think we both need some time to cool off.'

'Do we?' With a twist of his wrist, he pulled her towards him, taking her wrist behind his back, pressing it into the taut curve of his spine. Then, exerting an increasing pressure, he bent his head and covered her lips with his.

His kiss was electric. As soon as their mouths fused, a devastating weakness almost buckled her knees beneath her. A frisson of alarm slid down her spine, a warning that she had no defences where he was concerned. But then his tongue slid between her teeth and she couldn't bear to pull away.

Her lips parted beneath that sensual assault, and it was incredibly difficult to keep her eyes open when all she wanted to do was close them against the searching hunger in his. He was watching her, she thought fancifully, watching how easy it was for him to subdue her. But his predator's eyes were also hot and mesmerising, causing goosebumps to shiver over her flesh.

His mouth hardened, grew more demanding, and he released her wrist to place possessive hands on her hips. He drew her against him, letting her feel his heavy arousal throbbing against her stomach, leaving her in no doubt that, whatever his misgivings, he was as aroused as she was herself.

Tess's hands fisted at her sides for a moment, but the desire to touch him became irresistible. With a little moan of submission, she lifted her arms and linked them behind his neck.

His response was to urge her even closer, their bodies melding together from chest to hip. His hands burned on her thighs as he cupped her buttocks and lifted her against him, and she wound one leg about his calf as he rubbed himself against her.

The effect of that sexual abrasion was incredible. Tiny synapses of energy fused her nerves, ran unchecked under her skin. Her breasts felt tight and a tiny trickle of sweat ran down between them. She wasn't wearing a bra and she knew the dampness must be moistening the thin chemise top.

'*Tu voglio,*' he whispered unevenly, the roughening stubble on his jawline scratching her chin. His teeth fastened on the tender curve of her nape. She felt his suckling tongue right down to her core. 'I want you,' he repeated harshly, lifting his head to look down at her, his eyes darker now and strangely guarded as he met her startled gaze. 'And I am just crazy enough tonight to cast caution to the winds. So—if you have any doubts about this, stop me now.'

As if she could, Tess thought weakly. Her own needs were like a consuming fire inside her. She knew what he was saying, that he was taking all and promising nothing. But she doubted she had the will to resist him when this might be the only chance with him she had.

'I'm not a child,' she said, trying to sound blasé and failing dismally. 'I'm not a virgin either,' she added, as if he cared. 'You needn't worry about me. I—I know what I'm doing.'

Castelli's eyes softened. 'Do you?' he murmured, one hand curving over her cheek before slipping down to cup one firm rounded breast. Her nipple peaked, and he stroked his thumb back and forward across it. 'The question is, do I?'

Tess trembled, his caress causing a melting in her bones. But his words disturbed her, hinting as they did of some ambivalence on his part. With a convulsive swallow, she said, 'You're not having second thoughts, are you?'

Castelli shook his head, his hand finding the hem of her chemise now and sliding beneath it with unexpected ease. He watched her reaction as he touched the underside of her breast and then found the sensitive peak he'd been stroking earlier. And Tess thought how much more erotic his thumb felt against her bare skin.

She quivered then, leaning into him, and with a gruff sound he said, 'I am not made of ice, *cara*. Do you think I can touch you like this without wanting to see you also?' A trace of self-derision flickered in his eyes, but his expression didn't change. 'I may not know what I am doing. But I know I cannot stop myself. I have wanted you since the first day I saw you.'

Me, too, thought Tess fervently, though she didn't have the courage to say it. Instead, she stepped back from him and took his hand, linking her fingers with his. 'Would you like to see the bedroom?' she asked, amazed at her own temerity, and, with a sensuous narrowing of his eyes, he inclined his head.

It wasn't until she'd opened the door that Tess remembered she hadn't made the bed that morning. The sheet, which was all she usually used to cover her, was twisted, the pillows still bearing the indent of her head. Releasing his hand, she hurried to straighten the bedding. But Castelli caught her before she could do much more than pull the sheet aside and tugged her into his arms.

'Stop panicking,' he said, and she guessed he could feel her heartbeat hammering in her chest. 'We have all night,' he went on, dipping his head to nuzzle her shoulder. Then he brushed the straps of her chemise aside and drew it over her head.

It was hard not to feel some embarrassment as he stared at her. But her breasts were firm and high and she had no reason to feel ashamed of them. Nevertheless, she felt a quiver deep in her belly when he lifted his hands and cupped them almost reverently. And when he bent his head and buried his face in the moist hollow of her cleavage, she clutched the back of his neck and hung on for dear life.

When he lifted his head again, her face was flushed, damp strands of hair clinging to her neck and cheeks. He nudged her legs with one thigh and she parted them obediently. Castelli moved between them, rubbing sensuously against her sensitive core.

'You know we are wearing too many clothes, *fare lo non*?' he asked huskily, and, releasing her, he peeled his shirt over his head. Now her breasts brushed against the triangle of dark hair that angled down to his navel, hair that curled across his chest and shadowed his olive skin.

Tess stared. She couldn't help herself. She'd already guessed his body was taut and athletic and now she could see for herself. His nipples were pointed, his stomach flat and muscular, and below his navel another line of dark hair arrowed beneath the drawstring waistband of his pants.

The cord that hung from his waistband was irresistible. Before she could stop herself, Tess had reached out and pulled it free. Almost immediately, the soft trousers shimmied down to his ankles, and she was left to face the biggest erection she'd ever seen.

'You can touch me,' he said, kicking his trousers aside and tossing his deck shoes in the process. 'But do you not think we should lose these shorts first?'

His fingers easily disposed of her zip and the button that secured her waistband, but when he would have eased them down she grabbed the two sides in alarm.

'I—I had a shower when I came home,' she said. 'I—I didn't bother with any underwear.' She took a deep breath. 'Shouldn't we draw the curtains first?'

A glimpse of amusement touched his lean face at this evidence of her prudishness. 'Why?' he asked softly. 'Who can see us here?'

You can see me, Tess thought, releasing her hold on the shorts reluctantly. But what the hell? she thought. He was going to see her sooner or later anyway.

The denim cut-offs pooled around her ankles. Now it was Castelli who stared and she shifted uneasily under his gaze. *'Lei sono bello,'* he said hoarsely. 'You are beautiful, *cara*. Do not be ashamed of your body. It is *perfetto* in every way.'

Tess knew *perfetto* meant perfect, but she didn't believe him. She wasn't overweight, it was true, and her legs were slim, but she was a long way short of being ideal. Castelli on the other hand was magnificent. She wondered why he'd never married again. It was not for want of offers, she was sure.

'Now you help me,' he said, and her mouth dried instinctively. She wasn't used to such uninhibited behaviour and the idea of stripping his boxers from him was too much for her to take in.

But she did want to be close to him, and, hooking a finger into his shorts, she pulled him nearer. Which served the dual purpose of pretending to do as he asked and hiding her face as well.

'Ehi,' he said softly, gripping her waist and holding her away from him. 'Do not be afraid, *cara*. It will not bite.'

'I'm not afraid,' said Tess staunchly. 'It's just that I'm not used to—used to this.'

He gave a soft laugh. 'Oh, *amatissimo*,' he said, his voice rough with emotion. 'Do you think I do not know that by now? Here.' He took her hand. 'Let me show you. It will please me very much to be your tutor.'

He covered her fingers with his and used them to push his shorts down over his jutting manhood. It sprang free, thick and heavy and pulsing with heat. There was a smear of moisture at the tip that Tess found fascinating. She found herself itching to taste it and her breath came swiftly as he curled her palm around his silken length.

Her fingers moved automatically, and Castelli made a hoarse sound in his throat. Then his mouth was on hers again and she was pressed even closer and now there was no barrier between her and his naked frame.

Aching needs stirred inside her. She clung to him tightly, rejoicing in the freedom he had given her to do as she wished. His erection touched her mound and she arched her back instinctively. She couldn't wait to have him closer still.

When he released her mouth again, she made a sound of protest. But he swung her up into his arms and carried her to the bed. The cotton sheets were cool against her back as he came down beside her, and her legs parted almost involuntarily, inviting him to enter her and end her mindless need.

But instead of lying between her legs, he stretched out beside her, propping himself up on one elbow, seemingly content just to look at her. She shifted restlessly trying to let him see what she really wanted, but, although he obviously knew how she was feeling, he merely brushed her shoulder with his lips, his thumb brushing sensually over her mouth.

'Castelli—'

'Rafe,' he corrected her softly. 'My name is Rafe. I want you to use it. I am tired of being only Castelli to you.'

'Rafe, then,' she said obediently. 'Rafe—please! Don't you want to make love to me? I ache—' her hand flicked herself '—here; inside me. Do you know what I mean?'

'I have a faint inkling,' he teased her huskily, and now he bent and bit the soft skin above her breast. He tugged the flesh between his teeth and the feeling was erotic. Tess trembled violently. *Oh, God,* she thought, *I don't know how much more of this I can stand.*

But although she fretted beneath his hands, they were intensely pleasurable. While he suckled on her breast, his fingers trailed down over her stomach, raising little shivers as they went. They lingered in the hollow of her navel, then dipped into the curls at the apex of her legs. He was driving her to the brink and she was sure he knew it, could feel her essence hot against his hand.

He used his thumb to rub against the swollen nub of her womanhood, ignoring her protests as he inserted two fingers into her cleft. His fingers imitated the act of mating, and in no time at all she was writhing beneath him, far beyond the limits of her own control.

Her orgasm, when it came, was shattering, drenching him in moisture, bringing a look of raw satisfaction to his face. She wondered if this was all he wanted: to play with her without any real participation on his part. Then he removed his hand and replaced it with his mouth.

'No, please,' she said desperately, feeling herself responding again. Pleasurable as this was, it was not what she wanted. She pushed herself up on two elbows, trying to stop him. But Castelli only continued his sensual assault. She climaxed again, almost immediately, clutching his head instead of pushing him away.

He waited until she'd collapsed onto the pillows before moving over her. 'It was good, yes?' he asked huskily, and she tossed her head helplessly from side to side.

'It was good,' she agreed. And then, because she couldn't help herself, she reached up and ground her mouth against his with a tearful lack of restraint.

The kiss was as hot and passionate as before but he must have felt her tears against his cheek. He drew back to rest his forehead against hers and swore gently, frowning down at her. 'Why are you crying?' he asked softly. 'What did I do wrong?'

'You didn't do anything wrong. You just didn't do—anything,' she confessed unhappily.

She couldn't go on and Castelli captured an errant tear with the tip of his tongue. 'I told you,' he said. 'We have plenty of time. I am not going anywhere, *cara*. Relax. I just want you to remember tonight.'

He didn't say, 'When I'm gone,' but the words were implicit in what he had said. As if she would ever forget, thought Tess, with a wistful sigh. She wondered if she'd regret it when she got home, but that was not something she wanted to think about. This was a night out of time. A memory to console her in years to come.

He moved between her legs, positioning himself above her, but when she attempted to caress him with her lips he drew back at once. 'Not now, *cara*,' he said hoarsely. 'I am only human. And I want to be inside you when—well, you know what I mean.'

Tess didn't argue. She was desperate for him to be inside her, too, and she urged him on with real hunger in her eyes. She had been half afraid she wouldn't be able to take all of him, but her body stretched almost languidly, tightening about his length as he eased into her.

She felt a fullness then, a wholeness, a delicious anticipation of events still to come. And, although she'd been sure she couldn't be aroused for a third time, he soon proved that he was right and she was wrong.

She also realised the iron control Castelli must have been exercising over his emotions. He was breathing unevenly and his upper lip was filmed with sweat. His hands slipped beneath her bottom, lifting her against him. And when he began to move, the moist sounds their bodies made were sensuous to her ears.

'Dear God,' she moaned, giving voice to the wild emotions roiling inside her, and almost instinctively she wound her legs about his hips. She'd never dreamt she could feel like this, never dreamt she could be so uninhibited with a man. The inadequate experiences she'd had before had never prepared her for Castelli's lovemaking.

'Look at me,' he said once, causing her to gaze up at him with unguarded eyes. 'I want you to know who is with you. I want you to know we are together.' He looked down at where their bodies were joined, his eyes darkening with feeling. 'I don't want you to know where your body ends and mine begins.'

She nodded then, too emotionally aroused to use words to tell him how she felt. Instead, she reached up with her hands and pulled his face to hers, giving him her answer with her lips.

His movements quickened, and she felt her own emotions

spiralling upward. She hadn't believed she could feel anything so devastating after what she'd felt before. She looked at him again, saw the way his eyes grew unfocussed, and then reached that seemingly unattainable pinnacle as he found his release....

CHAPTER ELEVEN

TESS awakened next morning feeling a little sick and achy to the sound of someone hammering on the door.

She'd drunk too much wine the night before, she thought, half prepared to believe the hammering was in her head. But she knew her headache was just a minor symptom of what was really wrong with her, and, although she knew she ought to see who it was, she buried her face in the pillow instead.

Castelli hadn't left until it was almost daylight. They'd spent most of the night together, and, although they'd done very little sleeping, Tess had thought it was the most wonderful night of her life.

While she'd been recovering from their first bout of lovemaking, Castelli had gone into the other room and returned with the wine and two glasses. Comfortably at home in his skin, he'd knelt beside her on the bed, offering her wine and kisses, and the erotic delight of drinking it from his lips.

His uninhibited behaviour had been catching and pretty soon she'd been sitting up, knees drawn up to her chin while he'd reclined beside her. But then his hand had become too tantalisingly familiar, and they'd shared that incredible magic again.

They'd made love twice more, the last time as slow and languorous as she could have wished. Her body had been aching but it had been a sweet torment, and one that she would have willingly suffered for the rest of her life.

But that would not happen. She knew that. Had known it before she'd invited him into her bedroom. Castelli had given her no commitment, made her no promises. When he'd departed early this morning, he'd said nothing about seeing her again. And although she guessed they might have to be in contact when Ashley and Marco turned up, she didn't kid herself he'd find it difficult to walk away afterwards.

The hammering came again and she pulled the sheet over her head to shut out the sound. It didn't work, but it did shut out the morning sunlight streaming through the unguarded windows. Which reminded her anew of what had happened the night before. Making love by moonlight, the most romantic memory of all.

She knew she had to think about getting up and going to the gallery. She was still Ashley's deputy, at least until the beginning of next week. The fact that she would have been happiest to stay where she was for the rest of the day didn't figure. She was committed to doing what she'd been asked, even if no one else seemed to care about the rules.

Some people would say she'd been a fool, she thought ruefully. Ashley certainly would, if she ever found out. Her sister would never have behaved so recklessly, not without providing a safety net first.

Her sister!

Tess groaned. Oh, God, what time was it anyway? There was always the chance that Andrea might turn up as she'd threatened to do. She could imagine what her stepmother would say if she arrived and found Tess still in bed.

Pulling the sheet away from her face, she struggled up onto her pillows. Blinking, she managed to bring the clock on the bedside cabinet into focus. It was almost eleven, she saw with horror. She must have gone back to sleep after Castelli left. She had been very tired, but that was no excuse.

She could hear someone shouting now. The knocking was still going on, but it was accompanied by an angry voice calling her name. 'Tess,' she heard. 'Tess Daniels, are you in there? Will you unlock this door, dammit? I can't get into my own apartment.'

Ashley!

Tess's jaw dropped. And before she'd thought it through

she was halfway to the door. She remembered bolting it after Castelli left, never expecting anyone to try and get in with just a key. But then she remembered she wasn't wearing a stitch to cover herself with. Not even the man-sized tee shirt she usually slept in.

She and Castelli had slept in one another's arms, she recalled unwillingly, hurrying back into the bedroom to find her robe. Naked and unashamed, she thought, wondering why that now sounded so—so sordid. She grimaced. It was because Ashley had come back and now any chance of seeing him alone again had been removed.

She found her robe hanging on the back of the bathroom door and she slid her arms into the sleeves, wrapping it about her and tying the cord as she hastily retraced her steps. Ashley wasn't giving up and Tess guessed she'd been to the gallery first to find her. When Tess wasn't there, she'd guessed she must be here.

It wouldn't occur to her sister that Tess might have spent the night anywhere else. That she might have been to a party and been invited to spend the night. Despite what she'd told Silvio, Ashley wouldn't expect her to make friends here. Least of all…Tess arrested the thought. Castelli was not a friend.

'I'm coming, I'm coming,' she called now, half afraid the noise Ashley was making would encourage the old caretaker to call the police. She drew the bolt and turned the key, almost in unison. Then, pulling open the door, she said, 'I'm sorry. I slept in.'

'Didn't you just?' Ashley was not appeased by her apology. She strode into the apartment, looking about her as she did so, and Tess wondered if she suspected she wasn't alone. 'Get my case, will you?' she added, shedding a bulging backpack onto a chair. 'I've had to haul it all the way from the gallery. I expected you'd be using my car and I could collect it.'

'Sorry,' said Tess again, rather less meekly this time. But as Ashley went to fill the kettle and plug it in she obediently wheeled the case into the apartment, before adding, 'Perhaps if you'd told me that you were coming back, I could have arranged to pick you up at the airport.'

'There was no need.' Ashley was offhand, pushing her hair behind her ear with a careless hand. 'I got a cab from the airport. I thought you'd be relieved I was back.'

'Oh, I am.' As her sister stood there, casually making herself a pot of tea, Tess felt her temper rising. 'How is Andrea, by the way? I really ought to give her a ring myself.'

'Don't bother.' Ashley cast a wary glance over her shoulder and Tess wondered if she really thought she'd got away with it. 'She's okay. You know what she's like. Always exaggerating her illnesses.'

Tess pushed her hands into the pockets of her robe, feeling them ball into fists. 'You've spoken to her, then?'

Ashley looked at her again. 'Why?' Then, 'Of course, I've spoken to her.' She turned back to the kettle. 'What are you talking about, Tess? I've been staying with her for the past week.'

'Have you?' Tess steeled herself for the confrontation. 'That's funny. She says she hasn't seen you.'

'You've spoken to her?' Ashley swung round again, and this time her face was flushed with anger. 'What were you doing, Tess? Checking up on me? Dammit, now she's going to wonder what's going on.'

'As we all are,' observed Tess coldly. 'Did you really think I wouldn't find out? My God, Ashley, you never cease to amaze me.'

Ashley's mouth was sullen. 'You had no right to go checking up on me,' she declared. 'What did it matter to you where I was? You offered to look after the gallery while I was away.'

'You *asked* me to look after the gallery,' Tess contradicted her shortly. 'You told me your mother was ill and needed you. What a crock that was!'

'Well, you appear to have been having a good time anyway,' countered Ashley, gesturing towards her bathrobe. 'Obviously you haven't stuck to the letter of our agreement either. How often has the gallery stayed closed until lunchtime? That's my livelihood you're messing with, you know.'

'Oh, please.' Tess regarded her contemptuously. 'The gallery is the least of your problems and you know it.' She paused. 'Where's Marco? Did you drop him off at the villa?'

Ashley stared at her, open-mouthed. 'What do you know about Marco?' she demanded. Her brows drew together in a scowl. 'Oh, God, you've seen his father, haven't you?'

Tess felt sick. Until that moment she'd clung to the hope that there might have been some misunderstanding, that Ashley hadn't abducted Castelli's son and taken the boy away. But it was obvious from her sister's face that Marco had been with her. And like Castelli, she could only think the worst.

'Did you think the Castellis wouldn't try and contact you?' she asked now, incredulously. 'Dammit, Ashley, Marco's only sixteen!'

'He's almost seventeen,' said Ashley impatiently. 'Only his family doesn't seem to recognise that. They keep that boy in a glass case, Tess. No wonder he can't wait to break out.'

Tess blinked. 'So you decided to help him, did you?' she exclaimed bitterly. 'Whatever you say, whatever excuses you come up with, he is still only sixteen, Ashley. Did you honestly expect his father would approve of you—running off with him?' She shook her head. 'I thought you'd have had more sense.'

Ashley scowled now. 'What do you mean, running off with him?'

'Well, you did, didn't you? An investigator Cas—his father hired saw you get on the plane to Milan almost a week ago.'

'So?'

Tess gasped. 'So—where the hell were you going? You weren't on the plane when it got to Milan. They checked.'

Ashley looked mutinous for a moment and then she turned to make the tea and Tess was obliged to wait. What was she doing? Tess wondered. Concocting a convincing excuse or deciding how much to tell her? She didn't want to know all the intimate details. Heaven forbid! But she would like to know how they had avoided being found.

With the tea made and a cup poured to her satisfaction, Ashley crossed the room and sank down onto the shabby sofa with a sigh of relief. She sipped the tea, nodded appreciatively, and then turned to Tess again. 'Don't look at me like that,' she exclaimed. 'I'm not a pervert, if that's what you're thinking.'

Tess clenched her teeth. How could Ashley talk about what had happened so carelessly? She dragged a chair out from the table and perched on the edge, regarding her sister intently. 'All right,' she said. 'So tell me. What has been going on?'

Ashley shrugged. 'We've been in Genoa,' she replied, taking another sip of her tea, and Tess acknowledged that Castelli had been right about that, at least.

'But you bought tickets for Milan,' she pointed out, still waiting for an explanation. 'If it was an entirely innocent trip, why do that?'

'To put his family off the scent, of course,' said Ashley impatiently. 'We didn't want his father turning up and ruining his chance to get some real tuition for once.' She shook her head. 'His father won't even allow that he has any talent. When Marco told him he wanted to go on a painting holiday, he wouldn't even consider it.'

A painting holiday! Tess was nonplussed. 'And you think his father knew about this?'

'About his interest in painting? Of course.'

'No, not that.' Tess was impatient now. 'About this painting holiday or whatever it was? Because I don't think he did.'

'Well, Marco told him all about it,' asserted Ashley firmly. 'But we decided not to tell him where it was being held for obvious reasons. I didn't want him sending his goons after us.'

Tess caught her breath. 'I don't believe it,' she said incredulously and Ashley frowned.

'What don't you believe? That his family might have tried to stop us? Come on, Tess, you said yourself that Marco's father had hired an investigator to check up on him.'

'Because he was worried about him,' declared Tess vehemently. 'And whatever you believe, Marco couldn't have told his father where he was going. I doubt if he even mentioned a painting holiday to his family. When his father came to the gallery looking for you, he accused you of kidnapping his son!'

Now Ashley gasped. 'You're joking!'

'No, I'm not joking,' Tess retorted grimly. 'His family thinks you're having an affair.'

Ashley's face was difficult to read then. Tess thought she was dismayed. She hoped she was. But there was something strangely secretive in her expression.

Then she saw Tess watching her, and she shook off whatever she was thinking. 'You can't be serious,' she said, getting to her feet and striding across to the windows. 'For heaven's sake, Tess, what do you think I am?'

'So it's not true, then?'

'No.' But Ashley wasn't looking at her as she made the denial. She seemed to be intent on what she could see out of the window, the roofs of the small town and the harbour far below. 'You shouldn't believe everything you hear.'

'I'm only telling you what Marco's family thinks,' said Tess defensively, hoping Ashley wouldn't question how she came to be so knowledgeable all of a sudden. Now that her sister appeared to be exonerated, her own behaviour seemed even less justifiable.

Ashley turned then, wrapping protective arms about her midriff, causing the short skirt of her slip dress to rise high above her knees. She'd kicked off her high-heeled sandals when she'd come into the apartment, but her long legs were still shown to advantage. Tanned and slender, they complemented her shapely frame, making Tess feel small and insignificant beside her.

'Can I help it if that fool boy thinks he's in love with me?' she demanded suddenly, and Tess's eyes widened at this sudden shift in emphasis.

'You mean, you are involved with him?' she asked faintly, and Ashley gave her a scornful look.

'Haven't I just said I'm not interested in schoolboys?' she demanded. 'But that doesn't mean Marco doesn't have—expectations.' A slightly sensual smile tugged at the corners of her lips and Tess's doubts were rekindled. 'He's crazy about me, you know. That's why his father is so worried about him, I suppose.'

'Then what on earth possessed you to take him on a painting holiday?' protested Tess, disturbed by her sister's attitude. 'As soon as you realised how he felt about you, you should have kept out of his way.'

'Why?' Ashley was mocking. 'Just because his family don't approve?'

'Because he's only sixteen,' repeated Tess staunchly. 'For heaven's sake, Ashley, what are you trying to do? Alienate him from the Castellis completely?'

'That will never happen,' retorted Ashley positively, bending to pick up the cup of tea she'd deposited on the floor when she got up from the sofa. 'As you've obviously found out for yourself, Marco is the most important person in his father's life. He's a divorcee, you know, Signor di Castelli, and, according to Marco, he's got no intention of getting married again. So there'll be no other sons to pass on the family name.'

As if she didn't know, thought Tess painfully. But Ashley was waiting for her to say something and that definitely wasn't it. 'Do you know him?' she asked instead, which seemed a reasonable question. After all, Ashley would never expect Castelli to have shown any interest in her.

'I met him once, at the grape harvest last year,' her sister replied, confirming Castelli's comment. 'He's quite a hunk, isn't he? Or didn't you notice?'

'He's—quite attractive,' conceded Tess, realising that to say anything else would sound suspicious and Ashley gave her a scornful look.

'Quite attractive,' she mimicked. 'Tess, the man's gorgeous. Do you think I'd care what Marco's ambitions were if Rafe di Castelli was interested in me?'

She finished her tea and carried the empty cup into the kitchenette as Tess absorbed her last statement. But it wasn't what Ashley had said that really disturbed her. It was what she hadn't said that caused a shiver of apprehension to feather her spine.

'What do you mean?' she asked now, needing some further reassurance that she was mistaken. 'What does—Signor di Castelli have to do with you?'

'Can't you guess?' The face Ashley turned towards her was impatient. 'Oh, grow up, Tess, what do you think this is all about?' She rinsed out her teacup and set it on the drainer, drying her hands on a paper towel. 'I haven't wasted time on Marco just for his well-being. And if the Castellis want me to leave town when the gallery closes, it's going to cost them. That's all.'

Tess was appalled. But all she could find to say was, 'You know the gallery's closing?'

'Of course.' Ashley was complacent. 'I'm not stupid. The gallery's not making any money and Scottolino's no bleeding heart, believe me. He won't do anything to cushion my retirement. Not when I've only been working for him for less than a year.'

Tess swallowed as her aching brain kicked into action. 'And you think the Castellis will?'

'I'm sure of it.' Ashley nodded. 'I think they'll do almost anything now to get me out of their hair. Of course when I suggested this week at Carlo Ravelli's studio, I had no idea Marco would decide to keep the whole thing a secret. That's a bonus. I suppose I was surprised when there wasn't more opposition. But then nobody was supposed to know exactly when we were going.'

Tess stared at her. 'And don't you care that they were worried about Marco?'

'I'm sorry if I've upset anyone.' Ashley shrugged. 'But it's really not my fault. Besides, I don't owe the Castellis any favours. When Silvio took me to the villa last year—and that's some villa, let me tell you—the whole family behaved as if they were the aristocrats and the rest of us were just peasants!'

'Ashley!'

'Well…' A look of defiance replaced her complacency. 'It's true. They are an arrogant lot. All except Marco, that is. He and I hit it off immediately.' She smirked reminiscently. 'He came down to the gallery to see me the very next day.'

'And you encouraged him!'

'I didn't have to.' Ashley walked across to where Tess had left her suitcase and lifted the strap. 'I think I was the first person who'd taken his aspirations seriously. You've met his father and he has no time for his talent, and his grandmother treats him like a kid.'

'He is a kid.'

'He's a teenager,' retorted Ashley shortly. 'How many teenagers do you know who have to get their parents' permission to leave the house?'

'I'm sure that's an exaggeration.'

'Is it? You know nothing about it. I'm surprised Marco's father contacted you personally. He usually gets his assistant to do stuff like that.'

'Perhaps he was more worried than you thought,' remarked Tess, not wanting to get into her association with Castelli. 'Isn't it true that Marco has never shown any interest in painting before he met you?'

'Is that what his father said?' Ashley frowned. 'That must have been quite a conversation you had with him. What else did he say? Did he mention me at all?'

Tess had had enough. 'Does it matter?' she asked, getting up and wrapping her robe closer about her naked body. She needed a shower, she thought. She needed to check that Castelli hadn't left any visible marks on her skin. 'Perhaps you ought to ring your mother,' she went on, weary of the whole affair, including her part in it. 'She's been worried about you. I told her you'd ring as soon as you could.'

'Oh, yes. You went and grassed on me,' Ashley accused her grimly. 'Couldn't you at least have kept your suspicions to yourself?'

'I didn't grass on you,' retorted Tess. 'I told her I must have made a mistake about where you'd said you were staying. I didn't entirely drop you in it, though I don't honestly know why not.'

'Because you love me,' said Ashley at once, her expression lightening. She dragged her suitcase towards the bedroom. 'You know, it's good to be back. Now I'm going to have a long cool shower. I think I deserve it, don't you?'

Tess shook her head. 'What about ringing your mother?' she protested.

'Oh, I'll do that later,' replied Ashley dismissively. 'Why don't you get dressed and go and get us something for lunch?'

'Because I need a shower, too,' muttered Tess under her breath as Ashley went into the bedroom. But, of course, she'd have to wait. It was Ashley's bathroom, after all.

And it was then she remembered the tumbled bed and the empty wine bottle and glasses standing on the bedside cabinet. She had hardly time to register what her sister's reaction was likely to be before Ashley let out an angry yell.

'What the hell?' Ashley appeared in the open doorway again, brandishing the empty wine bottle, her face flushed and dark with anger. 'Who the—who have you had in here?' she demanded, practically flinging the bottle at her sister. 'And don't tell me you were drinking alone. The place stinks of alcohol and sex!'

CHAPTER TWELVE

LUCIA DI CASTELLI arrived at the villa soon after eleven o'clock that morning.

Rafe was in his study, trying to concentrate on the latest batch of sales figures, when his mother erupted into the room.

'I know where they are,' she announced triumphantly. 'I know what they've been doing. They're in Milan, at the home of some minor painter called Carlo Ravelli. He runs these semi-educational holidays. You know the sort of thing. People pay a certain amount of money for tuition and the rest goes on meals and accommodation. A house party, in effect, but one pays for the privilege.'

Rafe put his pen aside and looked up. 'I know,' he said evenly, and Lucia stared at him as if he'd suddenly grown two heads.

'You know?' she echoed. 'How do you know? How long have you known? If you've been keeping this from me—'

'I know because Marco arrived home half an hour ago,' Rafe interrupted her wearily. 'He and his companion flew back to Pisa this morning. He could have phoned and I would have gone to meet them. But they each chose to take a cab. He's upstairs right now unpacking his bag.'

His mother's jaw sagged and, groping behind her, she found a chair and dropped into it. 'Just like that?' she asked disbelievingly. 'The boy comes home and you have nothing to say to him? He disobeyed you, Rafe. He disobeyed both of us. Surely you're not going to let him get away with it?'

'I have no intention of cracking the whip, if that's what you expect,' Rafe replied civilly. 'Have you considered that it might be because we've been too hard on him that he feels it's necessary to rebel?'

'He's just a boy, Rafe.' Lucia was infuriated. 'When you were his age, you were still in school.'

'As is Marco,' Rafe reminded her. 'Just because I refused to let my son be educated in Rome, as I was, does not mean the college he attends locally is any the less adequate.'

Lucia pursed her lips. 'What you mean is, you had no intention of permitting Marco to train for the priesthood. You knew it was my dearest wish and you dismissed it out of hand.'

'Priests are born, Mama, not made,' retorted Rafe shortly. 'I can't honestly see Marco embracing the celibate life.'

'Well, not now, obviously,' muttered his mother. 'And what about this woman he went off with? Are you going to let her get away with it, too?' She snorted, and before he could reply she added angrily, 'We don't really know what they got up to, do we? Attending a course that's held in the home of an artist, of all things, can hide a multitude of sins.'

'I know that.' Rafe was irritated now, and he threw his pen down on the desk. 'Be assured, I will not allow Miss Daniels to get away with anything. Nor do I intend to make things easy for her.' He paused. 'Right now, she will be expecting me to turn up at the gallery, breathing fire. Instead, I shall do nothing for the next couple of days. It will do her good to—what is it the English say?—to stew for a while. Then, when I am ready, I will make my move.'

Lucia sniffed. 'And what is that move likely to be, exactly?'

'I don't know yet.' Rafe took a thoughtful breath and lay back in his chair. 'I have been asking myself what Miss Daniels intended to get out of this. Now that we know she was not lusting after Marco's body, it is an interesting question, is it not?'

His mother pursed her lips. 'How do you know she hasn't—I refuse to use that disgusting word you used—how do we know she hasn't seduced him anyway?'

'We don't,' said Rafe honestly. 'Except that Marco does not behave like a boy who has lost his virginity.'

'Raphael!'

'Oh, please.' Rafe sighed. 'Let's not use euphemisms here, Mama. Marco seems decidedly—subdued. As if—dare I say it?—he has been disappointed in love.'

'Well, that certainly sounds a lot better than losing his— um—innocence,' declared Lucia firmly. 'I just hope you are right and that Miss Daniels has the sense to leave him alone from now on.'

'I didn't say that,' said Rafe resignedly. 'I said I didn't think she and Marco had slept together, yet.'

'Yet?' His mother was scandalised. 'You can't think there's still a possibility of that happening, Raphael. He's home, apparently safe and sound. What more can she do?'

'I suppose that's what we're supposed to find out,' re-marked her son shrewdly. 'I don't think we've heard the last of Miss Daniels, Mama. That's why I say I intend to give her time to consider her options. It's always best to know your enemy. Attack isn't always the surest form of defence.'

Lucia grumbled some more but she eventually had to con-cede that Rafe was probably right. And besides, she was eager to tell him how she'd found out where Marco was.

'I went to the gallery myself,' she said, not noticing that her son's features had stiffened. 'I wanted to speak to her sister, but in the event she had nothing new to tell me. She insisted she didn't know where they were. Can you believe it? Anyway, I pretended to get upset and she invited me to recover in the office.'

Rafe's mouth compressed. 'Really?'

'Yes, really.' Lucia pouted. 'Don't look like that, Raphael. I have my methods, as you should know by now. Anyway, the stupid girl left me alone and I took the op-portunity to look through the drawers of the desk.' Her eyes sparkled. 'I found Ravelli's leaflet among a pile of similar leaflets for painting courses in various parts of the country. So I went to Pisa and saw your investigator, Signor

Verdicci. It was a simple matter for him to ring round all the agencies and find out if the Daniels woman had booked into any of them.'

Rafe breathed heavily. 'You took a leaflet?'

'I took several, actually,' said Lucia airily. 'Most of them in this area, as we knew they'd taken a flight to Milan. They're not of any value, Raphael. And if everyone had their rights, they probably belong to Augustin Scottolino. You needn't look at me like that. They don't belong to the Daniels woman, so don't fuss.'

'Nevertheless, you stole the leaflets,' said Rafe flatly, imagining how Tess would have felt if she'd discovered they were missing. 'You took advantage of Tess's kindness. And then left like a thief in the night.'

'How do you know I didn't put the leaflets in my handbag and leave like anyone else?' demanded his mother at once, and Rafe cursed himself for having a big mouth.

'Because I spoke to Tess yesterday,' he said. 'She told me you'd visited the gallery. She said you'd been upset, but she doesn't know you as I do.'

'Oh, don't be tiresome, Raphael.' Lucia regarded him impatiently. 'In any case, you seem to have become very friendly with this young woman.' Her disdain was evident. 'Have you forgotten that the woman who kidnapped your son is her sister, her flesh and blood?'

'I think we've established that no one kidnapped Marco,' Rafe retorted shortly. 'And, as I've said before, Tess is nothing like her sister.'

'How do you know?' His mother wasn't prepared to let it rest there, and Rafe guessed she was using his involvement with Tess to take the heat from herself. 'Because she says so?'

'Because she's a decent person,' said Rafe harshly, feeling an unwilling twinge of guilt at his own duplicity. 'In any case, we weren't talking about Tess, we were talking about your behaviour. I think you owe her an apology, don't you?'

As he'd expected, Lucia didn't linger long after that suggestion. His mother seldom apologised to anyone and she rarely admitted her mistakes. Although her own parents had only owned a *taverna*, she'd adopted her aristocratic bearing when she'd married Rafe's father, and over the years she'd put those humble beginnings out of her head.

Rafe sighed now, reluctant to admit that his mother's departure had resurrected his own misgivings. Although he'd felt tired and pleasantly sated when he'd arrived back at the villa, he'd known it was only a matter of time before his conscience reasserted itself. He'd managed to keep his thoughts at bay to begin with, and while he'd been dealing with Marco he'd had too much else on his mind. But the lethargy had cleared now and he was forced to face the truth of what he'd done.

The trouble was, he didn't want to acknowledge how he felt about it, felt about her. It was no use pretending he hadn't wanted to make love with Tess when, from the moment she'd opened the door in that thin camisole and skimpy cut-offs, it had been the only thing on his mind.

And before that, he admitted, deciding there was no point in trying to delude himself. He hadn't been lying when he'd said he'd wanted her from the first time he'd seen her. He realised now that that was why he'd been so hard on her in the beginning. Because at first he'd thought she was her sister—with all the baggage that had entailed. And later, because he'd realised that she could be dangerous to his peace of mind.

She was the first woman who had invaded his consciousness, to the extent that he couldn't get her out of his head. He thought about her, he dreamed about her, dreams he hadn't had since he was a teenager. He was worse than Marco, he admitted ruefully. Lusting after a woman he barely knew.

Yet it didn't seem like that when he was with her. There was a familiarity between them he'd never felt with anyone else. His obsession was such that he was able to fool himself that she wanted him, also. But, although they'd made love, he was no closer to finding out how she really felt about him. He should have had more sense and kept away from temptation. What was that he'd said about the perils of a holiday affair?

Ashley was outraged that Tess wouldn't discuss who she had been entertaining with her. She flounced into the shower, threatening all manner of reprisals, and Tess spent the time she was away changing the sheets and making the bed. The things she had done—like balancing the gallery's books and spring-cleaning the apartment—would mean nothing to her sister. As far as Ashley was concerned, Tess had behaved abominably and even the prospect of the revenge she intended to take on the Castellis was no compensation.

Not that Tess was anxious to have a heart-to-heart with her sister. Even talking about the gallery brought back too many painful memories of Castelli and the time they'd spent together. When Ashley emerged from the bathroom, Tess took a shower, too, albeit a cold one, and then dressed and went out to do some food shopping as Ashley had suggested.

She didn't mention the gallery. If her sister wanted to open up, that was her affair. After the way she'd behaved, Tess felt little responsibility towards her. She refused to feel guilty if the gallery remained closed all day.

When she returned to the apartment, she was half prepared for Ashley to have packed her bags in her absence. Tess had already faced the fact that she was unlikely to see Castelli again. If he went to the gallery, it would be Ashley he'd want to speak to, not her.

She entered the apartment in some trepidation. If Ashley was still here, there was no certainty that Castelli wouldn't be here, too. He might have come to the apartment, if the gallery was closed. She assumed he'd be eager to confront her sister with what she'd done.

But although Ashley was there, Castelli wasn't. Nor was there any sign that he'd visited while she was out buying lunch. However, to her surprise, Ashley's attitude had changed entirely. Instead of asking if Tess had booked her flight home, she astonished her by asking if she'd stay on for a few more days.

'I was hasty before,' she said, perching on a stool at the bar as Tess prepared a light meal of melon and ham and freshly baked rolls. 'I forget, you have your own life to lead. I guess I was jealous. Here I've been nursemaiding a love-struck teenager, and you've been getting it on with some sexy Italian.'

Tess winced. The description was too apt, and she couldn't avoid remembering how Castelli had cornered her in the kitchenette the night before. 'It doesn't matter,' she said, taking butter from the fridge and setting it on the bar beside her. Then, after adding knives and forks to the impromptu settings, she handed Ashley a plate.

'Thanks.' Ashley helped herself to salad before continuing. Then, after adding several slices of melon and some of the spicy ham to her plate, she lifted her head. 'This looks delicious, Tess. And I have to admit, I'm starving. They offered us coffee and rolls on the flight, but you know what airline food is like.'

Tess managed a slight smile and took the stool opposite. She didn't know what had caused Ashley's sudden change of heart, but she didn't trust it for a minute. Something had happened. Either Castelli had been here and Ashley thought she needed a bodyguard, or she'd found out who Tess had spent the night with and intended to use it to further her own ends.

'I'm not sure it's a good idea for me to stay on,' she murmured, after a minute's deliberation. 'I mean, you only have one bedroom and the apartment's really only big enough for one.'

'It's a double bed,' Ashley pointed out quickly. 'As I'm sure you were grateful for last night.' And then, perhaps because she thought that approach wouldn't win her any favours, she went on persuasively, 'You and I have shared a bed before.'

Tess pressed her lips together. The temptation to stay on for a few more days was attractive, but she was only kidding herself if she thought that seeing Castelli again was a wise thing to do. Wasn't it painful enough already? And did she really want to get involved in whatever scheme Ashley was planning?

'It's—kind of you to ask me,' she began at last, but Ashley interrupted her.

'You're not going to say no, are you?' she protested. 'Please, you've got to give me a chance to make amends.'

Tess shook her head. 'It's not that. I'm due back in school next Thursday,' she said. 'And I've got things to do, stuff to sort out, washing and so on, when I get home.'

'Then stay until Tuesday.' Ashley was persistent. 'You can do your laundry any time.'

'Ashley—'

'You've got to stay.' Ashley's tone had changed again and Tess regarded her warily. 'I need you. I can't handle this on my own.'

'You've handled things pretty well on your own up till now,' observed Tess, not inclined to be sympathetic. 'I don't want to get involved in this, Ash. We don't have that kind of relationship.'

'We never will, if you don't allow it to happen,' retorted her sister sulkily. 'What's wrong with you? I'm offering you a holiday and you're turning me down.'

'I'm sorry—'

'All right, all right.' Ashley hunched her shoulders and regarded her broodingly. 'There is another reason why I want you to stay on. I phoned my mother while you were out and she suggested coming out for a visit. I don't want her here now. God, surely you can see that? So I told her you were staying on and that I didn't have any room.'

'Ashley!'

'Well, it was all I could think of on the spur of the moment. And if you go back to England now, she's sure to find out.'

'How?' Tess blinked. 'We never see one another.'

'Oh, I don't know.' Ashley spread her hands expressively. 'I wouldn't put it past her to check up on you. Particularly after you'd rung to ask if I was there.'

'Which reminds me, did you tell her I'd suggested you'd take this job in Italy,' Tess asked, remembering Andrea's accusation.

Ashley shrugged now. 'I may have done.' And then, as Tess looked appalled, she tried to justify herself. 'You know the old lady always wants to know what I'm doing. As I couldn't afford to get a place of my own, it seemed a good idea to say you were in favour.'

Tess shook her head. 'You amaze me. You really do. Do you ever consider anyone but yourself?'

'Oh, come on, Tess, I'm not that bad really. Please, say you'll stay on.'

'But your mother won't get in touch with me. She knows you're back now.'

'Yes, but she's still suspicious. I had to tell her my mobile was out of order to explain why she hadn't been able to reach me.'

'And where did you say you'd been?' Tess asked. 'Just in case she asks me.'

'In Venice,' said Ashley offhandedly. 'I said Signor Scottolino had asked me to check up on one of his artists while I was there.'

Tess stared at her sister disbelievingly. 'The lies just roll off your tongue, don't they?'

'I think on my feet, that's all. As I say, I can't have my mother coming here.'

'And you really think a few more days will make a difference?'

'I'll think of something else,' said Ashley. 'I can always tell her I'm losing my job, remember? If I tell her I'll be flying back to England soon, she won't want to waste money coming here.'

'You are totally unscrupulous, aren't you?'

Ashley shrugged. 'I'd call it practical. You don't get anywhere if you don't assert yourself, Tess. But I don't expect you to understand.'

Yet she could. Tess bent her head over her meal, picking idly at a thin curl of ham. If she hadn't asserted herself last night, Castelli would have left without touching her. It was she who had decided to be self-indulgent for once in her life.

And staying on? Wasn't that another form of self-indulgence? She knew Ashley wasn't to be trusted. She ought to catch the next flight back to London and safety. It was foolish to think that she could exert any influence over her sister. And Castelli wouldn't forgive her for being a party to Ashley's deceit.

So why was she even considering her sister's offer? It wasn't for Ashley's sake. She'd meant what she'd said. Ashley could take care of herself. And she surely didn't think Castelli would want her sympathy. As soon as Ashley told him what she had in mind, he'd want nothing more to do with either of them.

'I'm sorry,' she said at last, her appetite deserting her. She pushed her plate aside. 'I don't want to get involved in your schemes.'

'You won't.' Ashley was definite. 'Why should you? Signor di Castelli will want to see me, not you. He'll probably come to the gallery tomorrow. You can be sunbathing on the beach while I deal with him.'

Tess sighed. 'Ashley—'

'Well, say you'll stay until Monday at least,' pleaded the younger girl persuasively. 'What's a few more days? You'll be doing me a big favour and what harm can it do? It's not as if you've booked your flight, and if I hadn't got back you'd be staying on anyway. One more weekend. Pretty please. Then you can go back to your old boring life in Buxton.'

Tess objected to her life being called boring. Though she had to admit that, compared to the life Ashley led, it did seem rather dull. But safe, she reminded herself firmly. And predictable. These few days in Porto San Michele had been exciting, but she preferred a more secure existence.

Didn't she?

CHAPTER THIRTEEN

IN THE event, Tess couldn't get a flight until Tuesday. It was nearing the end of the Easter holidays and all the flights were fully booked. As it was, she was only on standby, and she had been asked to ring the airport Tuesday morning to check availability. The booking agent seemed to think that she would make it, but Tess was less convinced.

She refused to think what she'd do if she couldn't get a flight before Thursday. She could imagine what Mrs Peacock, her head teacher, would say if she wasn't back for the start of the new term. Mrs Peacock lived and breathed for East Vale Comprehensive, and unfortunately she expected her staff to do the same.

Ashley, of course, was delighted. Although her delight was decidedly muted by the end of Monday when she hadn't heard from either Marco or his father.

'They're keeping him away,' she said angrily, storming into the apartment after the gallery had closed, her face flushed with frustration. 'Well, they needn't think they're going to get away with it. I'll go to the villa, if I have to. Marco has a right to see whoever he likes.'

'It's not Marco you want to see, though, is it?' Tess remarked shrewdly. 'If you ask me, you've been lucky that his father hasn't contacted the police. Taking a minor away from his family is probably an offence here, just as it is at home.'

'That's rubbish!' Ashley didn't want to hear Tess's argument. 'Marco came with me of his own free will. His father knows that as well as you do.'

'All the same...'

'All right, all right. You may have a point. But that still

doesn't alter the way Marco feels about me.' She frowned as she considered her options. 'Somehow I've got to see him, to talk to him. Maybe if you could get in touch with his father—'

'No!' Tess was adamant. 'I told you I didn't want to get involved in your schemes.'

'And you won't be.' Ashley gazed at her appealingly. 'Come on, Tess. All you have to do is ask him to come to the gallery. I'll take it from there.' She spread her hands. 'I think you owe me. You were so determined to leave, but you're still here, enjoying my hospitality. I could have thrown you out.'

'No.' Tess turned away, and as she did so she heard someone knock at the door. She stiffened, her mouth going dry. 'I—I think you've got a visitor.'

'At last!'

Tess barely had time to conceal herself in the bedroom before Ashley had the door open. She tried not to listen, but she couldn't deny the longing she felt to hear Castelli's voice again. But the voice was younger, lighter, definitely not a man's voice, and her spirits sank accordingly. Marco, she thought dejectedly. Ashley would be rapt.

She sat down on the bed, expecting a long wait, but only moments later the door opened. Ashley came into the room, carrying a white embossed envelope. 'It's for you,' she said shortly, tossing it at her sister. 'A delivery boy brought it. It's got the vineyard's logo on the back. So, tell me, why would Signor di Castelli be writing to you?'

Tess's stomach hollowed. 'I don't know,' she said. And she didn't, although she doubted Ashley would believe her. She turned the envelope over, curiously reluctant to open it with her sister standing there, watching her. 'Ms Teresa Daniels,' she read, half disbelievingly. Yes. It was definitely for her.

'Open it,' said Ashley irritably, unaware of her ambivalence. She had no way of knowing that the letter filled Tess with a mixture of expectation and dread. She'd thought she'd dealt with her feelings for Castelli, but the way she felt about this letter proved she hadn't. And she dreaded the disappointment she was sure was to come when she read it.

'Hurry up,' Ashley persisted. 'It's probably about me. I want to know what lies they're telling about me. And how did they know you were still here?'

'Well, I didn't tell them,' said Tess, resenting the implication, though that thought had occurred to her, too. She ran a nervous finger under the flap and eased it open. 'I have no idea why—why any of the Castellis would write to me.'

'Just open it, Tess.' Ashley was impatient. She waited with obvious agitation for her sister to pull the sheet of notepaper out of the envelope. Tess did so, unfolding it with shaking fingers. 'Well?' the other girl prompted. 'What does it say?'

Tess read the words once, then read them again, hardly able to believe what she was seeing. 'I—we're—invited to dinner at the Villa Castelli,' she said weakly. 'The invitation's for tomorrow night.'

'Really!' Ashley didn't bother to curb her sarcasm, leaning over Tess's shoulder and reading the letter herself. 'What do you know? An invitation to the villa! I told you they'd want to see me again.'

Tess shook her head. 'Well, I can't go.'

Ashley scowled. 'Why not?'

'Because I'm going back to England tomorrow,' replied Tess steadily. 'According to the airline, I should be able to get a seat on one of the afternoon flights.'

'You can't be serious!' Ashley stared at her disbelievingly. 'If you think I'm going to lose my chance to speak to Marco's father just because you think getting back to your prissy job in England is more important, you're mistaken.'

'I'm not stopping you from going,' protested Tess defensively.

'It was sent to you. How will it look if you don't turn up?'

Tess told herself she didn't care. That even the thought of going to the villa filled her with trepidation. She didn't know why Castelli had invited them, but she doubted it was going to be a social occasion. The mention of dinner was just a lure, an incentive to Ashley. He had no intention of allowing her to get away with what she'd done.

'I can't go,' she repeated now, folding the letter again and pushing it back into the envelope. 'I've got to get back to England. I can't afford to lose my job.'

Ashley was desperate. 'If you go, I'll never forgive you,' she said threateningly. 'I'll—I'll do something terrible to myself and I'll make sure my mother knows that you're to blame.'

'Then do it,' said Tess wearily, too distressed to care if she was hurting the other girl's feelings. 'Ashley, if you think I'm going to the villa knowing that you intend to ask for money, forget it. I've supported you this far but no further.'

'Tess!'

Ashley's wail of anguish was drowned out by the ringing of her mobile phone. The strains of Beethoven's 'Moonlight Sonata' sounded incongruous in the small apartment, but Ashley had evidently come to the same solution Tess had and she hurried into the other room to find the phone.

'Marco?' Tess heard her say excitedly. And then, 'Oh. Oh, I see. Yes. Yes, she's here.' By the time Tess had reached the bedroom door, Ashley was already coming back to her. 'It's Marco's father,' she hissed, with her hand over the mouthpiece. 'If you blow this, Tess, I'll make sure you regret it.'

Tess pulled a face at her as she took the phone. But her hand was shaking and she guessed Ashley attributed it to what she was threatening to do. 'H-Hello,' she said. And then, refusing to let Ashley intimidate her, she closed the door in her face. 'Signor di Castelli?' She moistened her lips. 'What do you want?'

'Oh, *cara*, is that any way to greet a lover?' he mocked gently, and she was tempted to disconnect the call there and then. He had no right ringing her here, no right to send her invitations to the villa. Just what game was he playing? Divide and conquer?

'I received your invitation,' she said tersely, deciding now was as good a time as any to tell him she wouldn't be accepting it. 'I'm sorry, but I'm flying back to England to-morrow.'

'Surely not.' His voice was low and disturbingly familiar. It couldn't help but stir the memories she was trying so hard to forget. '*Cara*, I want to see you again. Do not tell me you do not wish to see me also.'

Tess's breath came unevenly. 'I think the person you want to see is Ashley,' she said, keeping her voice steady with an effort. 'And—and she wants to see you, too, so that's all right. I—don't want to get involved. It's nothing to do with me. I've got to get back to England. I—I'm sorry if this disrupts your plans, but I think it's the best way, don't you?'

Castelli sighed. 'I cannot believe you can dismiss the night we spent together as if it never happened,' he said softly.

'It shouldn't have happened,' Tess responded, her palms becoming moist at the thought.

'No?' He sounded regretful. 'Me, I do not believe that. I remember every moment of it, *cara*. How it felt to touch you, how it felt to be inside you—'

'Stop it!' Tess couldn't bear to listen to any more knowing he didn't mean it. This was just a ploy to get her to agree to accompany Ashley to the villa, so she'd be there to pick up the pieces when he blew her sister apart. 'I—we agreed there were no commitments, on either side. It—it was—fun, but it didn't mean anything. You know that.'

'You wound me, *cara*.' His voice sounded strangely

harsh now and she guessed he hadn't expected her to see through his deception. 'And we did not agree to anything, as I recall. All I told you was that I was not prepared to offer you a holiday affair.'

'Nevertheless…' Tess felt out of her depth, but she refused to let him persuade her that the night had meant something to him when for the last three days she'd heard nothing from him. 'I know you're just using me to get at Ashley. Well, she can take care of herself. She doesn't need me to hold her hand.'

'You are perhaps concerned because you have been having some difficulty in getting on a flight back to England,' he went on, as if she hadn't spoken.

'How do you know that?' she demanded, but he didn't answer her.

'You are afraid you will not be back in time to start the new term at your school.' He paused. 'I can personally guarantee that if you accompany your sister to the villa tomorrow evening, you will be flown back to England the following day.'

Tess gulped. She would not be manipulated like this. 'No!'

'*Molto bene.*' Very well. His tone had hardened now and when he spoke again there was no expression in his voice. 'If you persist in adopting this attitude, then I am forced to take sterner measures.' He sucked in a breath. 'If you will not accept my invitation, then you leave me no choice but to contact the police.'

Castelli had said he would send a car for them and the sleek black limousine arrived promptly at half past seven. Tess had thought of arguing, of saying that as Ashley had a car they could drive themselves to the villa, but she decided not to bother. What was the point? Whatever she said, he'd do what he wanted. For the first time she was beginning to see what Ashley had been dealing with.

Not that she could forgive her sister for getting her involved in this. Not even Ashley's assertion that Castelli deserved everything he got was any compensation at all. But her sister was right about one thing: the Castellis were a law unto themselves. If they wanted something, they got it, and despite Ashley's confidence she doubted this was going to be an easy few hours.

Nevertheless, Ashley had been delighted when Tess had told her she was going to the villa, after all. She didn't care about all the murky details, the fact that Castelli had practically threatened them with arrest if they didn't obey his orders. Such things meant nothing to her.

'He'd never do it,' she said, when Tess voiced her own doubts about the proceedings. Then, judging that her sister might change her mind, Ashley added, 'Well, he might. I suppose we can't give him the chance, can we?'

In consequence, Ashley had spent all the next day searching for a suitable dress to wear that evening. She'd suggested that Tess should do the same, but she'd refused to waste time and money on such an event. She was convinced the whole evening was going to be a disaster. Why should she get dressed up?

As she was applying a bronzed eye-shadow to her lids, however, she half wished she'd done as Ashley suggested. There was no doubt that the white sheath her sister was wearing gave her the confidence of knowing she looked her best. And Ashley did look good, tall and slim and darkly beautiful. She made Tess feel like a pale shadow of herself.

Now, sitting in the back of the limousine, Tess accepted she could never compete with Ashley. Although she'd abandoned her first choice of a long skirt and basque top in favour of a black slip dress, she still felt underdressed. Her bare legs were nicely tanned, but they bore no comparison to Ashley's, which were much longer. And where Ashley's hair was smooth and sleekly styled, Tess's was a spiky blonde halo around her head.

It was about thirty kilometres from Ashley's apartment to the Villa Castelli. The chauffeur, a man of middle years, wearing a navy blue uniform and a peaked cap, informed them it would take about half an hour.

'No speeding tickets for him, then,' whispered Ashley drily, pulling a face at her sister. But after experiencing some of the hairpin bends on the road, Tess had to admit she was relieved.

And, no matter how prepared she'd thought she was, the Villa Castelli was so much more than she'd ever imagined. It seemed to float above a valley, where the mist rising from a lake that was hidden among trees gave it an eerie insubstantiality. The purpling shadows of evening were massing behind it, looking like mountains in the fading light. It was beautiful and remote, more like some fairy-tale palace than a house.

'What do you think?' asked Ashley in an undertone as the chauffeur turned between stone gateposts and they started up a steep, curving track towards the villa. They drove between cypress trees and flowering oleander, the vineyard dropping away below them in terraces where the budding vines would eventually ripen in the sun.

'It's—impressive,' said Tess, aware of the inadequacy of her words. 'Do you think so?'

'You forget, I've been here before,' Ashley reminded her. 'Not to go inside, I grant you. But I was pretty stunned by the house and grounds.'

'Hmm.'

But Tess was feeling more and more apprehensive. The beauty of the place, its very atmosphere, was intimidating, and no amount of encouragement on Ashley's part was going to make her feel any different. She didn't belong here; they didn't belong here. She felt like one of the Christian prisoners must have done before they were thrown to the lions.

'That's the loggia at the side of the house,' Ashley pointed out as they drew nearer to their destination. 'Marco and I had a glass of wine there. He was showing me the view.' She gave an expressive sigh. 'He's quite sweet, in his own way.' She lifted her shoulders. 'I could get used to living like this, you know.'

Tess glanced half apprehensively at her. 'That's not why we're here,' she warned, half afraid the younger girl was thinking of changing her mind.

'I know that. But I can dream, can't I?' Ashley retorted. 'In any case, I'd probably get bored after a while.' She pulled a face. 'But the money would be nice.'

Tess shook her head, dreading the evening before her. She felt as if she was dealing with three—or possibly four— people all of whom had their own agenda. How did Marco feel about his father's intervention? What kind of reception had he received when he'd got home? And would Signora di Castelli be there, casting a malevolent eye over the proceedings? Had she told her son about her visit to the gallery? Or was Tess supposed to behave as if she'd never seen the woman before?

So many questions; so few answers. The car was slowing and Tess felt totally unprepared for what was ahead. For the first time in her life she wished she could be more like Ashley. Her sister was enjoying this. She was actually looking forward to going head-to-head with Castelli himself.

The first impression Tess had was of grace and elegance. As she stepped out of the car beneath a pillared portico she was instantly enchanted by the building's sun-bleached walls and sloping roofs. A long veranda, made bright with hanging baskets and planters filled with flowering shrubs, gave access to a lamp-lit foyer, where more flowers sat in vases or spilled from urns across the floor.

The floor of the foyer was tiled in a rich pattern of white and gold and navy, and set about with chairs and sofas in matching shades. White walls, archways supported by sculpted columns, and yet more greenery, overflowing from pots and climbing up the walls.

A uniformed manservant had met them on their arrival, and it was he who escorted them inside. Then, with a murmur of apology, he left them to let his employer know that his guests had arrived, and Tess was left to wonder again why she had ever agreed to this.

Beyond the foyer a splendid apartment invited inspection. But although Ashley peered into the room, Tess remained firmly where she was. She could see enough: polished maple floors, soft hide sofas, chairs upholstered with tapestries embroidered by an expert hand. There were tall cabinets filled with artwork, low tables and oriental rugs. And raw silk drapes at the long windows that faced a huge fireplace with a carved marble surround.

It was the home of a rich man, thought Tess ruefully. As if she hadn't known that already. Was that why Ashley had been invited here? Because Castelli wanted to intimidate her with his wealth? Not that she really believed he needed any assistance. He was a master manipulator. She was here tonight because he'd insisted she should be. Instead of flying home to things that were familiar and safe, she was standing here waiting for the proverbial axe to fall.

Footsteps sounded on the stairs that led down into the foyer and she turned her head abruptly. But it wasn't Castelli who appeared. It was a much younger man. He was tall and slim, dressed in an open-necked white shirt and navy pants, and he looked so much like his father that Tess knew this must be Marco.

'Hey.' It was Ashley who spoke first, going to meet him as he reached the hall. 'What about this place?' she said, apparently realising he didn't look particularly pleased to see her. 'I had no idea it would be so—grand.'

'Didn't you?' Marco's smile came and went so swiftly Tess almost missed it. But then he was turning towards her, his hand extended in greeting. 'You must be the other Miss Daniels,' he said. 'My father asked me to come and meet you. Unfortunately, he has had to take a phone call. He will join us shortly.'

Tess allowed him to shake her hand, and then said, 'It's Marco, isn't it? You look so much like your father, I can't be mistaken.'

'Of course, this is Marco.' Ashley didn't like being ignored and she immediately went to his side and slipped her arm through his. 'Are you okay, sweetie?' she asked, deliberately attempting to invoke an intimacy between them. 'I hear you didn't tell your father about our trip.'

Marco looked down at her momentarily, a curious expression playing about his mouth. 'No, that was a mistake,' he said, politely removing himself from her possessive hold. '*Adesso*, will you come with me? There are drinks waiting on the loggia.'

Tess could see that Ashley liked this even less. Her dark brows drew together and she looked decidedly put out. For her part, Tess had to wonder if her sister had been mistaken about Marco's infatuation for her. Unless, the painting holiday—or his father—had opened his eyes.

CHAPTER FOURTEEN

THEY bypassed the elegant salon and entered another reception room, with a high frescoed ceiling and a cool marble floor. The furnishings were a little less formal here: cane-backed chairs, painted tables, cool statuary between windows that were open to the air. Mesh screens prevented insects from investigating the tall lamps that stood beside a grand piano, but Marco pushed them aside to allow them access to the loggia beyond.

The first person Tess saw was Lucia di Castelli. As Marco closed the screens again she saw Castelli's mother watching them from the comfort of her chair. She was not alone, however, and the elderly gentleman sitting with her rose to his feet politely. Unlike Marco, he was wearing a velvet dinner jacket and Tess hoped this wasn't going to be a very formal occasion.

His smile was welcoming, however, unlike Lucia who looked decidedly put out. *'Chi e questo?'* he said, speaking to Marco, and the boy quickly made the introductions.

'This is an old friend of my *nonna's*. The Count Vittorio di Mazzini.' He glanced at Tess and then continued. 'These are the two Miss Daniels we were telling you about, Tio Vittorio.'

A count! Tess digested this as the old man bowed over her hand. *'Piacere, signorinas,'* he said. And then continued with less fluency, 'Welcome to Italy. You are enjoying your visit to San Michele?'

'Tess is visiting. I live there,' remarked Ashley, before Marco could explain the situation. Her gaze moved to the other occupant of the loggia. 'And you must be Signora di Castelli, Marco's grandmother. Am I right?'

158

Tess winced at the brash way her sister had insinuated herself into the conversation and Lucia got regally to her feet. 'I am Lucia di Castelli, yes,' she said. 'Do I take it you are the young woman who works for Augustin Scottolino?'

The omission of any other reference was conspicuous. In those few words, Castelli's mother had successfully removed any connection between Ashley and her grandson. Tess could see the count absorbing this, perhaps wondering why the Castellis should have invited them to the villa. But he was too polite to ask the question and Lucia patted his hand understandingly.

'Are you not going to offer our guests some refreshment, Marco?' she asked as Ashley fumed over the deliberate slight. 'I hope your father will not be too long. It seems cooler this evening. Do you not think so, Vittorio?'

The count nodded as Marco said, 'That was my intention, Nonna.' He gestured towards the tray of drinks on a cabinet close by. 'What would you like, Miss Daniels?' He addressed himself to Tess again. 'Would you like wine, or a cocktail? Or perhaps you would prefer something stronger.'

'I think Tess would like wine, Marco,' remarked another voice behind them. Tess turned to find Castelli closing the screen door. 'White wine, am I right?' he asked, causing Ashley to transfer a wide-eyed gaze to her sister. Then, 'I am sorry I was not here to greet you. My *avvocato*—my lawyer—called at just the wrong time.'

Tess didn't know whether the mention of his lawyer was deliberate or not. She didn't know what to think with him standing there staring at her with that intent searching gaze. Another ploy? she wondered. Another gambit? Another attempt to put both her and Ashley on their guard? What was Ashley thinking? Was this what she had expected? Tess rather doubted it, but you never could tell.

'It doesn't matter,' she said now, realising they were all waiting for her to answer him. 'And—and a glass of wine would be very nice.' She paused, and then continued bravely, 'But I'd prefer Chianti. White wine tends to give me a headache.'

Ashley's eyes narrowed at this and Tess realised that she hadn't been too wise. It had been an empty bottle of white wine that Ashley had found in her bedroom. Now all it needed was for her sister to connect the two.

'Veramente?' Tess was glad it was getting dark and she hoped only she had noticed the sardonic arching of his brows. *'Bene, Marco. Chianti per la signorina, per favore. E Ashley? Un bicchier di vino, sì?'*

'No, thanks.' Ashley spoke offhandedly, and Tess wondered what she thought she'd achieve with that attitude. 'I'd prefer a gin and tonic, if you have it. Just show the gin the tonic, Marco. You know how I like it.'

The insinuation was plain and Tess accepted her glass from Marco and turned away. Lucia and the count had resumed their seats and were talking together, so she moved to the edge of the loggia, ostensibly to admire the view.

Even in the fading light, the lake glimmered below them like a jewel set among the trees. Stars were winking out and the sky grew darker as a sliver of moon appeared. A moth swooped past, bent on its own destruction, its destination the dozens of candles that illuminated the terrace.

'Do you like it?' murmured Castelli, and she realised he had come to stand beside her. He was wearing black trousers and a black silk shirt this evening and his sleeve, rolled back over his forearm, brushed her skin. If she was surprised he chose to make his interest in her so plain, she chose not to voice it. This was just another way to anger Ashley, she thought. He wanted her to bring the battle to him.

'It's beautiful,' she replied coolly. What else could she say? He had probably been complimented by more sophisticated guests than her. She moistened her lips and then decided there was no point in avoiding the issue. 'Why have you brought me here, Signor di Castelli? And please don't insult my intelligence by pretending you wanted to see me again.'

'But I did,' he told her softly, turning and propping his hips on the stone balustrade. 'And my name is Rafe, as I've told you several times already.' She could see his face now, his tawny eyes darkening and smouldering with an emotion she didn't want to identify. 'Come on, *cara*, say you are pleased to see me. Is this not a more civilised way of spending an evening than exchanging insults?'

Tess shook her head, her wine forgotten. 'I don't understand,' she said, wishing he wouldn't look at her that way.

'You will in—what is that expression?—in the fullness of time, *no*?' He lifted his hand and rubbed her arm with proprietary familiarity. 'You are cold. Would you like to go inside?'

'What I'd like is for you to stop treating me like an idiot,' she blurted in an undertone. 'You have no right to touch me, no right to—to jerk me around to satisfy some perverted desire to score points.' She swallowed, setting her glass aside, admitting that she really had no love for Chianti. 'Why have you invited Ashley and me to dinner? I know— I just know you don't really want us here.'

'I want you here,' he contradicted her, his voice playing on her senses. 'If to achieve that I have to be civil to your sister, also, then so be it.'

'No.' Tess was insistent in her denial. 'Dammit, you know nothing about me.'

'But I want to know more,' he essayed smoothly, his words rippling across her flesh. 'I want to possess you, *cara*. Not just your body, no matter how delectable the experience was, but your soul also.'

Tess trembled. A film of dampness enveloped her. Her stomach contracted and tiny beads of moisture trickled between her breasts. Did he know how she was feeling? Of course he must. He'd done this before. But she hadn't, and she was agitatedly aware that she was out of her depth.

A breeze wafted the scent of pine onto the loggia, and the draught of air stirred her awareness of his warmth, his heat. Despite what she'd said, she recognised the scent of his aftershave. It was as familiar to her as the clean male aroma of his skin.

She wondered if his sensual words had had an effect on his emotions. Though she had to remember that a man didn't need to involve his emotions to become aroused. Nevertheless, the thought took root, a disturbing compulsion she had to fight against. Much as she wanted to, she didn't dare let her eyes drop below his waist.

She had to get away from him, she told herself unsteadily. Before she did something really stupid like grab a handful of his shirt and jerk him towards her. Or maybe she would lean forward and wrap herself around him. Wouldn't his mother get a surprise if she did something as outrageous as that?

'Do it,' he urged her huskily, and she realised she had been staring at him for fully half a minute. And, dear God, it seemed he really could read her mind.

'Go to hell,' she snapped, grabbing up her glass again and marching back to where Ashley was still talking to Marco. Though, judging by her sister's expression, she was no happier with their conversation than Tess had been with his father's.

Marco seemed pleased to see Tess, however, and immediately asked if she wanted another drink. 'Nothing else, thank you,' she replied as Ashley turned to look accusingly at her. 'I'm not usually much of a drinker. I only have a glass of wine now and then.'

'Except when she has male company,' observed Ashley maliciously, finishing her own drink and offering her glass for a refill. 'Isn't that right, Tess? Even you have been known to break your own rules.'

Tess felt a wave of colour rising up her throat. 'I expect so,' she said, not wanting to argue with her in this mood. 'You have a beautiful home, Marco. Did this view inspire your desire to paint?'

'Oh, I would not say so,' murmured the boy, busying himself with replacing bottles on the tray.

'Marco's decided he doesn't have what it takes to become a painter,' Ashley put in scornfully. 'Or perhaps his father has decided for him. Who knows?'

'Marco knows that if he wants to continue with his painting studies, he has my permission,' declared Castelli, strolling across the loggia to join them. 'But now, I suggest we go and have dinner. Antonio has been trying to attract my attention for the last ten minutes.' He gestured towards the screens. 'Shall we go inside?'

To Tess's relief, there was no formal gathering to go into the house. Castelli led the way, with Ashley and Marco following on behind. The two older people made up the rear, and Tess was grateful when the count spoke to her about England. It was easier to think of going home and the enormous relief that would be.

The dining room they used was smaller than she'd expected, though she guessed it wasn't the only dining room in a house of this size. Nevertheless, its partly panelled walls and many small paintings made it less imposing, a huge chandelier suspended over the ebony table highlighting silver cutlery and Venetian glass.

The chandelier wasn't lit, however. Instead, silver candleholders, set at either end of the table, flickered with a mellow light. Scarlet hibiscus set among dark shiny leaves provided an exotic centrepiece and red wine, poured into tall decanters, looked rich and dark.

The table was set for six and Tess was relieved to find that Marco was sitting beside her. Castelli and his mother occupied the places at either end of the table, with Ashley and the count opposite. It should have been a pleasant occasion, but Tess was full of tension, a headache threatening at her temples. Only the count seemed unaware of the atmosphere—and Castelli, himself, who seemed able to divorce himself from any situation.

The food was exquisite: tortellini, filled with parsley and ricotta; tender chicken sautéed in a lemon sauce. There was a green salad to cleanse the palate before a selection of rich pastries and Italian cheeses were offered, and as much wine as she could drink, which wasn't very much.

In fact, Tess ate very little either. She was conscious of both Castelli and his mother watching her, and Ashley was obviously nurturing her resentment as she kept allowing the man who served them to refill her glass. Tess hoped her sister wouldn't drink too much and say something that would embarrass them all. Castelli's surprising acknowledgement of his son's interest in painting had evidently rankled.

Marco spoke little, answering his grandmother when she asked how soon he had to return to college, and exchanging the occasional few words with the count. When Ashley spoke to him, he seemed strangely noncommittal, and Tess could see that her sister resented his detachment.

Just as Tess was beginning to hope that they might get through the meal without a scene, Ashley turned to her host and said, 'I suppose you think you're very clever, don't you?'

'Ashley!'

Tess was appalled. Clearly the wine had loosened her sister's tongue and she dreaded what she might say next.

But, although Lucia di Castelli looked mildly dismayed, Castelli was unperturbed. 'Not clever at all,' he demurred, getting up from the table. 'But if you wish to speak to me, I would prefer it if you did not embarrass my guests.'

'I bet you would.' Ashley made no attempt to get up from the table, and Marco cast his father a worried look.

'I think Ashley's had too much wine,' he said, and Tess admired his courage for saying it. He looked across the table at the younger woman. 'Would you like to get some air?'

'With you?' Ashley drawled, narrowing her eyes suggestively, and Tess wanted to die at that moment. She had guessed this was coming, but there'd been nothing she could do to stop it. She just hoped Marco had more sense than to play into her sister's hands.

'Yes, with me,' said Marco, pushing back his chair and getting to his feet.

'But perhaps I'd prefer to be escorted by your father,' Ashley declared, apparently deciding Marco wasn't going to give her what she wanted. 'How about it, Signor di Castelli? Would you like to show me the gardens by moonlight?'

'Papa!'

'Ashley!'

Marco and Tess spoke almost simultaneously, but Castelli was already helping Ashley up out of her chair. 'I will be delighted to show you the gardens, *signorina*,' he said, 'if your sister will agree to accompany us.'

Tess looked up then, right into his eyes, and her heart felt as if it turned a somersault right there in her chest. Oh, God, she thought, why was he doing this, why was he tormenting her? Why didn't he just tell Ashley he wasn't playing her games and send them home?

'I don't need a chaperon, *signore*.' Ashley swayed a little and caught his arm and Tess almost groaned with frustration.

But, 'I do,' was all he said in reply, and once again he was looking at her. '*Bene*, Tess,' he said. 'Will you come with us?'

Tess pressed her lips together for a moment, and then she nodded and got abruptly to her feet. 'If you insist,' she said, refusing to acknowledge the angry stares Ashley was casting in her direction. This wasn't her choice, surely her sister knew that.

'Shall I come, also, Papa?'

Marco was obviously disturbed by this development and Ashley gave him a contemptuous look. 'Oh, yes,' she said scornfully. 'Why don't we make this a family party? Are you coming, Lucia? Count? Let's all go outside and have ourselves an orgy.' She gave a harsh laugh. 'That sounds like a plan.'

Tess was mortified, as much by Ashley's disrespect towards the older woman as by what she'd actually said. She'd had no idea that the wine would have such an unfortunate effect on her sister. She seemed totally out of control.

Castelli said nothing. He merely took Ashley's arm and guided her across the room. It was only when Ashley tried to jerk away that Tess realised her sister wasn't cooperating. But as Tess knew for herself, Castelli was immensely strong.

'Papa...'

Marco spoke again, and Tess could see that the boy was unsure what to do in the circumstances. 'Order coffee,' said his father without pausing. 'Tess! Are you coming?'

What choice did she have? thought Tess, casting an apologetic look at Castelli's mother and the count. Then, 'Excuse me,' she said, ducking her head, and hurried after the others.

Once again, they emerged onto the loggia, but this time Castelli led Ashley down the steps to the formal gardens that surrounded the house. The night air was cool and lightly scented with orange blossom. Tess thought she would never encounter that smell again without thinking of tonight.

But at least the night air seemed to bring Ashley to her senses and lamps, set among the greenery, illuminated their path. When they were far enough from the villa for their conversation not to be overheard, she succeeded in wrenching her arm from Castelli's grasp. Then she glared at both of them with equal dislike.

'What is this?' she exclaimed. 'What do you know that I don't, Tess? You insisted you didn't want to come here, so I don't think you're involved in this conspiracy. Or are you?'

Castelli took a deep breath. There was a stone fountain close by and he leaned back against the rim. 'There is no conspiracy, Miss Daniels,' he declared after a moment. 'I thought it was important that you should hear what Marco has to say. I have not threatened him and I am not threatening you. I have been extremely tolerant. And your sister is here because I invited her. I wanted her to know exactly what was said between us.'

'Oh, really?' Ashley sneered. 'What are you afraid of, *signore*? Don't you think you're big enough to handle a red-blooded woman like me?'

As Tess cringed at Ashley's crassness their host shrugged indifferently. 'I have no desire to handle you at all, Miss Daniels,' he remarked and Ashley's face flushed with anger at his dismissal. 'But I do not trust you. You are, I think, quite unscrupulous in your desire to achieve your own ends.'

Ashley snorted. 'It sounds as if you think I might charge you with assaulting me,' she retorted. 'That's not a bad idea, accusing the arrogant Raphael di Castelli with rape.' She looked at Tess, whose mouth had dropped with horror. 'How do you know she won't support me? Just think how much more convincing it would be if we both told the same story.'

'For pity's sake, Ashley!'

Tess started to protest, but Castelli's words overrode her. 'Tess wouldn't do it,' he said. 'And I think even you have more sense than that. This is not a game, Miss Daniels. It is my son's life you have been toying with. And I should tell you, you are only here now because I have no desire to hurt your sister.'

Ashley's eyes narrowed. 'So Tess is involved.' She made a contemptuous sound. 'I might have known it. What has she been telling you? That I wouldn't touch your darling boy, if I had a choice.'

'I've said nothing,' Tess exclaimed, stung by Ashley's willingness to shift the blame onto her shoulders. 'Let's go home, Ash. Can't you see you're wasting your time here?'

'Not yet.' It was Castelli who spoke now and they both turned to look at him. 'I think it is time I came to the point of this discussion.'

'I wish you would.' Ashley ignored her sister. She parted her lips and allowed her tongue to appear in silent provocation. 'Poor Marco will be wondering where I am. Just because he's decided he doesn't have a talent for art doesn't mean we can't still see one another. He's been a little subdued this evening. I think it's time I showed him how to have some fun.'

Castelli's lips curled. 'I think Marco has realised he made a mistake going away with you,' he said levelly. 'He tells me you and this man, Carlo Ravelli, got to know one another rather well.' Tess caught her breath and turned to her sister, but Castelli wasn't finished. 'Marco is not a fool, Miss Daniels. You may have thought you were very discreet, but he is not too young to notice what was going on.'

Ashley looked furious now. 'Are you saying that little rat was spying on me?' she demanded.

'Not spying on you, no.' Castelli shook his head. 'But, as I am sure you have told your sister, Marco was infatuated with you. Do you blame him if he was concerned that Ravelli was becoming too familiar? He wanted to protect you, Miss Daniels. He thought the man was annoying you. Imagine his surprise when he found Ravelli slept in your bed.'

Tess was stunned, and even Ashley looked a little sick at this revelation. 'He was mistaken,' she said hastily. 'Carlo was just—just pretending he was interested in me.'

'Oh, I believe you.' Castelli was sardonic. 'I imagine a man like Ravelli makes many conquests. You were just one more. But you made a mistake, too, Miss Daniels. Just now, when you said Marco would be missing you, you knew he would not. A young man's feelings are easily hurt. And you hurt Marco. You made a fool of him, *signorina*. He will not forgive you for that.'

'You mean, you won't let him,' snarled Ashley, and Tess knew she could see all her carefully thought-out plans going down the drain. 'Well, we'll see, Signor di Castelli. I'm not planning on going anywhere. Marco may change his mind when I explain it to him.'

'I do not think you will have time to explain anything to

Marco. You will not be staying in San Michele, Miss Daniels,' he declared, spreading his hands. 'As of tomorrow, the gallery is to be closed. I have spoken to Augustin Scottolino and I have his word on that.'

'You—you—'

'Careful, *signorina*. You have not heard all that I have to say and you may regret it if you are too reckless in your anger.' Castelli glanced at Tess briefly, and then went on with heavy emphasis. 'I am prepared to make your—what shall we say?—your redundancy more tolerable. If you agree to leave San Michele and return to England, I will pay forty thousand pounds into your bank account. Not all at once, of course, but in instalments: ten thousand pounds a year for the next four years.'

CHAPTER FIFTEEN

TESS was teaching a year nine class when Mrs Peacock sent for her. One of the school secretaries came to give her the message and Tess felt an immediate sense of apprehension. Mrs Peacock did not drag one of her teachers out of class unless something pretty drastic had happened. Had either Ashley or her stepmother been taken ill or involved in an accident? Heaven forbid! If not, she couldn't imagine that she'd done anything wrong.

Not that she could be absolutely sure of that. Although the private jet the Castellis had provided had ensured that she'd been back home in plenty of time for the start of term, Mrs Peacock had chided her for being unavailable for the whole of the holidays. She had tried to get in touch with her, she'd said. Certain assignments hadn't been handed in before the end of term, and the head teacher had decided to make it her business to find out why. The fact that Tess had been able to assure her that she had all the assignments and was marking them hadn't pleased her. Particularly as Tess had had to admit that she still had some marking left to do.

All the same, that had been over three weeks ago. Since then, Tess had done everything she could to complete her work on schedule and keep out of Mrs Peacock's way. This summons now was really depressing. She was beginning to think she hadn't been cut out to be a teacher, after all.

Looking after the gallery in San Michele while Ashley was away had probably unsettled her, she decided. It had been an emotional roller coaster from start to finish and even now she couldn't think of what had happened without regret. Regret for Marco, who had discovered firsthand what it felt like to be betrayed, and for herself in allowing Ashley to ruin her life.

Pursing her lips, she hurried along the corridor towards Mrs Peacock's office. That was over-dramatising things, she told herself. Ashley hadn't ruined her life; she'd done that for herself. She'd known from the beginning that it would be madness to get involved with Rafe di Castelli. Yet, she'd let him get close to her; had encouraged him, in fact. And when the inevitable had happened and he'd made love to her, she'd allowed herself to fall in love with him.

And how pathetic was that?

The only blessing was that Ashley hadn't guessed how stupidly she'd behaved. Even with the evidence of the wine bottle and the fact that some man had spent the night in the apartment, Ashley hadn't associated that with him. Or perhaps she'd had more important things on her mind when they'd got back from the villa. Like how soon she could start spending Castelli's money. And how she could now afford to rent a small flat in London instead of living with her mother.

For her part, Tess had been too disgusted at the turn of events to make much conversation, and she guessed her sister had assumed she was to blame for Tess's black mood. And, in part, she was. Tess had been sickened by the way Ashley had accepted Castelli's offer. No wonder he thought money could buy anything. Yet, he was to blame, also. She found it hard to forgive him for making her an unwilling witness to her sister's greed.

He'd tried to speak to her after Ashley had gone back to the house to collect her belongings. He'd blocked her path when she'd tried to follow her sister, saying desperately, 'Please: do not go like this.' And when she still refused to speak to him, to look at him even, he became angry. '*Dio mio.* Tess,' he burst out. 'What did you expect me to do?'

'I don't want to talk about it,' she told him stiffly. 'I don't see any reason why you had to involve me in this sordid affair.' She darted a glance his way and then wished she hadn't when she saw the haunted look on his face. 'Were you really afraid that Ashley might accuse you of assault if you spoke to her alone? Or did you just want me to see for myself how ruthless you can be?'

'Ruthless? No!'

He seemed stunned by her accusation. And she guessed that in his world what he'd done was no big thing. Paying off a mistress was probably acceptable. And if Ashley hadn't actually been Marco's mistress, that didn't matter. In fact it was a plus, and it still got her off his hands.

'Cunning, then,' she said, refusing to feel any sympathy for him. 'Giving Ashley the money in four instalments. I suppose you're hoping that by the time Marco is twenty-one, he'll have more sense than to get involved with her again.'

Castelli sighed then. 'I do not believe Marco would be so foolish as to care what your sister does, with or without the money,' he said flatly. 'And if your sister was the only one involved, I think I would have taken that chance. I am not buying Marco's freedom, Tess. I was hoping I was making the problem of Ashley go away, for both of us. And I knew it would be easier if she thought she had won.'

Tess didn't know what to think then, except that he was cleverer than even she had imagined. Somehow, he'd turned the situation around and made it seem as if he'd done it all for her. As if, she thought bitterly. How could he even imagine she would condone his behaviour? He was powerful, and ruthless, as she'd said, and he was determined to have his own way.

Somehow, she pushed past him then and hurried along the path back to the villa. Ashley was waiting and Signora di Castelli was happy to summon the chauffeur to drive them back to Porto San Michele. Only Marco seemed to care that his father wasn't there to bid them farewell. But Tess put his concern down to anxiety that their plan might not have worked.

Since then, Tess had spent many sleepless nights wondering why she'd been so eager to think the worst of him. Perhaps the truth was, it had been the only way she knew to get out of there without breaking down completely. Whatever he'd said, whatever he'd done, she'd known there was no future in their relationship. Allowing he had only had the best interests of all concerned at heart only made it impossible to bear.

Outside the corridor windows, it was raining. A steady drizzle had fallen for most of the last week, which hadn't helped. East Vale, which lay on the northern outskirts of Buxton, was a pretty place, and Tess used to like living here. But now her job had become her only lifeline in a future that stretched ahead of her, cold and bleak.

Mrs Peacock's office door stood ajar and Tess halted rather uncertainly. The older woman was a stickler for protocol and her door was always shut. She usually made her staff knock before being summoned into her presence. Tess thought it gave her a feeling of importance and that usually worked to her advantage.

Now Tess tapped at the door, only to find it opened inward at her touch. 'Mrs Peacock?' she said, half alarmed at this development. Surely the woman wasn't ill. She would hardly have sent for Tess if she were.

Her alarm increased at the sight of a man standing by the window. He had his back to her and, for a moment, she wondered if he was an intruder. But there was something unbelievably familiar about the way his dark hair brushed the collar of his leather overcoat, a disturbing recognition that she knew him.

'Come in, Tess,' he said, without turning, and her mouth dried at the realisation that it was Castelli. She'd thought it might be; no, she'd known it *was*. What she couldn't get her head round was why he should be here.

'Um—where's Mrs Peacock?' she asked. A stupid question, but it was the only thing she could think to say. The real questions like, *Why are you here? What do you want?*

were simply beyond her. She had neither the courage, nor the right, she conceded, to ask him anything.

'She has gone to organise some coffee,' he said, and now he turned to face her. The incongruity of that statement, the fact that Mrs Peacock never organised coffee for her guests herself, went over Tess's head. She was staring at him, noticing how much thinner he looked, the lines beside his mouth that hadn't been there before. 'How are you, Tess? You look well,' he continued, his hands pushed deep into his pockets. His lips twitched as he looked at her, too. 'You are letting your hair grow.'

Tess put an uncertain hand to her head. Then let it fall to her side. 'I—yes. Yes, it used to be long, but I cut it before—before the Easter holidays.' She moistened her lips. 'How are you? How's Marco? Your mother?'

'Marco is back at school, working hard, I believe. My mother?' He shrugged. 'She and Vittorio have gone on a cruise.' He paused. 'Me, I am surviving. I think that is the expression.'

Tess let out the breath she had hardly been aware she was holding. And then, realising she was still hovering in the doorway, she stepped rather tentatively into the room. 'Surviving?' she said, not sure how to take that and deciding he was probably being sarcastic. 'I'm sure you're in no danger of extinction.'

'You think not?'

His words disconcerted her and for a moment a wave of fear swept over her. 'You're—you're not ill, are you?' she asked, moving to the desk and staring at him across its width.

'Would it make any difference to you if I was?' he countered, making no attempt to leave his position by the window.

She tried to gauge if he was serious. Then, 'Of course it would,' she said, feeling her nails digging into her palms at her side. She swallowed. 'But you're not ill, are you? That was just a trick question. What are you doing here, Castelli?

If you're looking for Ashley, I've told you she doesn't live near me.'

His dark face hardened. 'I did not come here looking for your sister,' he said harshly. '*Dio*, Tess, must every conversation we have include that woman's name? At the risk of being ridiculed again, I came to see you. My assistant and myself had no easy task to find you. Do you know how many schools there are in the Buxton area? I can tell you, more than a few.'

Tess glanced nervously behind her. She had left the door to the corridor open and she could imagine Mrs Peacock coming back and hearing this and wondering what on earth this annoying member of her staff had done now.

'She will not return,' said Castelli, as if reading her mind. 'We are alone, Tess. Now—perhaps you will tell me how you felt when you discovered I was here.'

Tess took a deep breath. 'I—I was surprised,' she murmured inadequately.

'Surprised?' His dark brows arched in inquiry. 'So, you do not hate me any more?'

'I never hated you.' The words broke from her. 'I never said I hated you.'

'But you did not like me much when you left the villa,' he reminded her softly. 'I have found it very hard to live with that.'

Tess felt a quiver in her stomach. 'I'm sorry,' she said, not knowing how to answer him. Had he come all this way to gain her forgiveness? It was probably the kind of thing he would do. 'I—I think after what happened, I just felt— humiliated. But—but afterwards, I understood that you thought you were protecting your son.'

Castelli swore then, dragging a hand out of his pocket and raking it across his scalp. 'My son can take care of himself,' he said harshly. 'It was you I was concerned about. That was why I wanted to make sure you did not leave Italy until I had had a chance to speak to you. You seemed so—

loyal, so vulnerable. I wanted you to see how unscrupulous your sister was and—in your terminology—I blew it.'

Tess really didn't know what to say now, and she could only shake her head helplessly. It was obvious he blamed himself for what had happened and she wished she had some trite reassurance to give him.

'It doesn't matter,' she said at last. 'I've gotten over it.' She pressed her hands down on the desk, trying to keep the emotion out of her voice. 'Um—are you staying in England long?'

Castelli blew out a breath. 'That is the question, is it not? How long am I staying?' His lips twisted. 'What shall I say? As long as it takes to persuade you to come back to Italy in the summer?'

Tess blinked. 'Well, I would like to visit Italy again,' she began, but he interrupted her.

'Perhaps I did not make myself plain,' he said. 'I want you to come back to Tuscany and stay at the villa with me.' He paused as her eyes widened, her lips parting in confusion. 'Marco is spending the summer in France, working at a vineyard in the Loire Valley. We will be completely alone and, if that scares you, I will ask my mother to act as chaperon.'

Tess could only stare at him. 'Why would you want me to stay at the villa?'

Castelli didn't answer her. Instead, he went on, 'Lucia is already of the opinion that I am crazy to think you might agree. She says you only see me as Marco's father, that I am too old for such nonsense. And I know she is right, but still I had to come.'

Tess drew a trembling breath. 'Why do you want me to stay at the villa?' she asked again. 'Castelli—Rafe—what exactly are you offering? A holiday in the sun, or some crazy compensation for what you think I think about what you did for Ashley?'

He bent his head, his lean cheeks hollowing as he composed his answer. 'I am offering neither,' he said, his voice rough with emotion. 'It is my unskilled way of asking you if you will give me another chance.'

Tess was really trembling now. 'Another chance for what?' she asked unsteadily, needing him to spell it out, and he lifted his head, his face haggard in the grey morning light.

'To show you how much I care about you,' he said simply. 'To give me time to prove I am not the arrogant fool you think I am.'

Tess couldn't believe what she was hearing. And some of that confusion must have shown in her face. But this time Castelli's sixth sense was sadly lacking. Because instead of understanding how she was feeling, he carried on.

'If—if you think I am too old for you, as my mother says, then I would have to agree with you. Or there may be some man in England who has a prior claim to your affections. If there is, then so be it. But you understand I had to come here. I had to know—'

'Don't!' Tess cared about him too much to allow him to continue. 'Please, Rafe, don't go on.'

'No?' His eyes darkened, their tawny brilliance clouded now and dull with fatigue. '*Bene*, at least that is honest.' He made an obvious effort to gather himself. 'Perhaps you would give my thanks to Mrs Peacock for allowing me to use her office.'

'No, you don't understand!' Before he could move, before he could talk himself out of the room and out of her life, Tess had to stop him. She sidestepped the desk as he came towards her, virtually forcing him into a partial retreat. 'Oh, God, Rafe, I thought I was never going to see you again.'

He looked stunned now, staring at her as if he couldn't quite believe what he was hearing. He lifted his hands as if to grip her arms and then let them fall. 'You mean, you will come to the villa?' he asked hoarsely. And when she nodded she saw that the hand he raised to grip the back of his neck shook a little.

It made her want to touch him. It made her want to take hold of him and silence any doubts he still had with her mouth. Even the idea of kissing him again caused an explosion of need in her belly. She'd wanted him so badly, she realised. Could she really believe he wanted her, too?

'You—you will stay for how long?' he probed, and she wondered what he was thinking.

'How long would you like me to stay?' she countered softly, knowing that as she spoke her warm breath was fanning his chin. She'd stepped closer so that there was barely a hand's breadth between them. The sides of his coat were parted and she felt his heat envelop her despite the fine silk of his shirt.

'For ever,' he suggested harshly, and then shook his head as if impatient with himself. And, before she could respond, he changed his answer. 'Um—you have six weeks' holiday, do you not? If I say four weeks—'

Tess could hardly speak. He actually wanted her to live with him at the villa. Any limitations to be put on it, she would put there herself. She took a breath, knew that the next few minutes were probably going to be the most important minutes of her life. With a daring she hardly recognised she said huskily, 'For ever sounds better.'

Castelli made a strangled sound in his throat. 'You mean—you want to stay with me?'

'As long as you'll have me,' she whispered, lifting her hand to cup his cheek. 'Is that what you wanted to hear?'

'*Dio, mi amore,* it is what I wanted to hear,' he said, his voice breaking with emotion. He covered her hand with his and turned his face into her palm. She felt his tongue against her skin, shivered in anticipation. And then he bent his head to hers and his mouth touched her lips.

Tess clutched the front of his coat, pressing herself against him. She could feel his heart hammering in his chest, sensed the wildness in his kiss that he was trying so hard to control. But he was hungry for her; they were hungry for each other. And what began with sensitivity and tenderness quickly developed into a passionate assault that seared her soul.

He stepped back, taking her with him, and with the wall to support him he transferred his hands to her breasts. Her nipples peaked at the first brush of his fingers over the white blouse she was wearing, and she desperately wanted him to pull the hem of the blouse out of her skirt and touch her skin.

The scratch of his stubble scraped her cheek as he explored her earlobe, his teeth catching the soft flesh and dragging it into his mouth. Tess felt consumed by her senses, at the mercy of her body's gnawing hunger, and when he finally pulled away she gave a plaintive cry.

'Rafe—'

'*Cara*, I want you,' he told her fiercely. 'How can you doubt it? But not here. Not in this office.' He gave a half-smile. '*Per di pui*, I think that would be too much for your Mrs Peacock, *no*?' He ran his tongue across her parted lips to console her before putting her from him. 'Come, show me where you live. You said you had an apartment, did you not?'

Tess's apartment occupied the ground floor of a Victorian town house about half a mile from the school. To her surprise, she discovered Castelli had leased a car, a small compact, much different from the cars he drove at home.

'I know the Peak District a little,' he said as they covered the short distance to Hawthorn Terrace. 'I did some potholing here when I was a young man.'

'You're still a young man.' Tess hesitated for a moment and then squeezed his thigh with unfamiliar intimacy. 'I still can't believe you're real, that you've actually come all this way just to see me.'

'Not just to see you,' Castelli corrected her softly. 'To tell you I want you in my life.'

Tess had her keys in her hand as they went up the short path to the entrance of her apartment. But her hands were trembling so much, she couldn't open the door. Eventually, Castelli took the keys from her and succeeded in unlocking it, and then they were inside and she turned automatically into his arms.

The kiss they exchanged was all too brief before he gently nudged her ahead of him down the long narrow hall. 'Show me where you live,' he said, and she led the way past the bedroom and the living room into the kitchen-cum-dining room, keeping up a rather breathless patter as they went.

'I've lived here for almost nine years,' she said as he paused in the doorway to the kitchen. 'I'm responsible for the décor. I painted it myself. And do you like my plants? I grow herbs because they have such a lovely scent.'

'It is—charming,' he said, and, although she knew it was much different from what he was used to, she had the feeling he meant it. 'I have tried to picture your home many times in my imagination.' His smile came and went with a gentle sweetness. 'I knew it would be as neat and efficient as you.'

'You make me sound very dull,' she said, turning away to switch on the concealed lights to brighten the small apartment. She wasn't sure of him any more, she realised. Bringing him here had probably been a mistake. The kiss they'd exchanged had hardly been the passionate encounter she'd envisaged. There seemed to be a hesitation between them now, which she didn't know how to breach.

But while she was fretting over this, bustling about, filling the kettle and setting out cups for instant coffee she doubted he'd like, he came behind her. He had shed his coat, she discovered as he slipped his arms about her waist.

'*Cara,*' he said huskily, 'there is nothing dull about you. You are everything I have ever wanted in a woman. But are you prepared to give up your life in England to come and live with me?'

Tess caught her breath. 'I thought I'd already proved that,' she exclaimed, twisting in his arms until she was fac-

ing him. She framed his face with her hands. 'I'll do anything you want. You know that.'

'But it is a big step,' he said, and she acknowledged it
was when he was obviously making no formal commitment.
What had Ashley said? That Marco had insisted his father
would never get married again?

'If you want me, I'm yours,' she said simply, casting any
lingering doubts aside as she gazed up at him. If she lived
with this man for a year, or a month, or a week, it could
never be enough. But she would take what she was given
and be grateful for it.

'*Mi amore!*'

Castelli's hoarse words of endearment were his submission. His mouth sought hers as his hands pressed her even
closer to his taut frame. The feel of him, the smell of him,
the taste of him surrounded her, and she tore his shirt apart
and burrowed next to his skin.

'*Dio*, Tess, these have been the longest three weeks of
my life,' he muttered, unbuttoning her shirt with unsteady
fingers. He exposed the lacy bra she was wearing, and a
look of pure indulgence crossed his lean face. '*Bellissima,*'
he said, bending to bury his face into the moist hollow between her breasts. 'You are so beautiful, *innamorata*.'

Tess trembled beneath his hands and even Castelli
seemed a little shaken by the strength of their feelings for
one another. Glancing behind him, he saw one of the dining
chairs pulled out from the table and sank down into it with
obvious relief.

He had taken her with him, and she could feel his erection
hard beneath her now. Hitching up her skirt, she straddled
him to bring him even closer to the pulse that was beating
between her legs.

Castelli had loosened her bra and his teeth tugged almost
painfully at her nipple, but she knew it was only an indi-
cation of how desperate to be with her he was. His shirt
was open now and she peeled it off his shoulders, running
her tongue over his warm flesh, revelling in the taste of him.

Touching him like this was such a turn-on. So much so that she couldn't resist unbuckling his belt and unzipping his pants.

'Tess,' he groaned, but he didn't stop her, though when she started to caress him he had to protest. 'Remember I am only human and I want you very much,' he said thickly. 'Unless you do not want me inside you when I come you had better not touch me any more.'

Tess hesitated only a moment, and then, sliding off his lap, she quickly dropped her skirt and panties to the floor. 'Is this better?' she breathed, positioning herself and then sliding down slickly onto him, and Castelli caught her mouth in a savage kiss.

'*Molto meglio.* Much better,' he said hoarsely, and with a triumphant little smile she rose above him again.

'And this?' she whispered as his hands clung to her hips to guide himself deeper into her, and he nodded and buried his face between her breasts, unable to speak.

It was soon over, and when they were both weak and breathless from their passion Castelli sealed their lovemaking with a tender kiss.

'*Ti amo.* I love you,' he told her huskily, making no attempt to separate himself from her. 'I want you to come back to Italy with me. I cannot wait for another two months to elapse before you are free.'

EPILOGUE

THREE months later Tess was quite used to living at the Villa Castelli. Marco seemed quite happy to have her around and, although Maria still had reservations, because Tess had made her father so happy she was prepared to give her the benefit of the doubt.

Castelli's mother was another matter. Tess knew she didn't approve of her son living with a woman who was not his wife. But, like Maria, she had had to accept that Rafe was obviously in love with his English mistress, and Tess guessed she thought that in time he'd get tired of her as he had of other women he'd dated.

For herself, Tess didn't look too far to the future. It was enough that she was here, that Castelli apparently doted on her. She certainly doted on him, and if at any time the prospect of what she would do if he became tired of her impinged on her consciousness, she determinedly fought the demons of that particular despair.

Travelling back to Italy with him had been so exciting. At first she hadn't known how Castelli had persuaded Mrs Peacock and the board of governors to let her leave halfway though the term, but eventually he'd confessed that he'd made a donation to the school, a fact he'd kept from her, he'd said, because he'd been afraid she wouldn't approve.

Which had been rather foolish, she'd conceded, kissing him. That was one occasion when she'd been grateful for his financial contribution. Giving up her apartment had been harder. But, as Castelli had said, there'd been no point in continuing to pay rent when she wasn't coming back.

Well, not immediately, she amended now, waking to find the bed empty beside her. She and Castelli had their own

183

suite of rooms and she slid out of bed and padded naked into the bathroom without any fear of being observed. Who knew what the future held? She had already stayed longer than she knew her stepmother had expected. Andrea had been very scathing when she'd explained what she was going to do.

Ashley was in the United States at present. Although she, too, had been scornful of Tess for giving up her teaching post and moving to Italy, she was too busy with her new career in advertising to care. Tess suspected what she was doing was not quite as glamorous as she would have them believe but she wished her sister every success anyway.

Tess was in the shower when she saw a shadow in the bathroom, and she wasn't surprised when, moments later, Castelli slid open the shower door.

'I hoped you would not yet be up,' he said, and she saw he was just wearing his boxers. 'I went downstairs to get something out of the safe.'

Tess turned off the shower and stepped out into the folds of the fluffy towel he was holding. 'I thought you'd gone to work,' she said. Castelli spent most mornings in his office at the winery, and Tess had got into the habit of giving English lessons to the children whose parents worked on the estate while he was away.

'It is Saturday,' he said, and she pulled a face at the realisation.

'I'm still half asleep,' she confessed ruefully. 'That's why I was taking a shower.'

'We will both take a shower later,' said Castelli, walking back into the bedroom, and Tess followed him, feeling an anxious tingling in her stomach. He hadn't kissed her, she thought. He hadn't made any attempt to touch her after wrapping the towel around her. Another morning he would have joined her in the shower. Was something wrong?

His words came back to her. He'd been downstairs, he'd said, getting something out of the safe. Oh, God, she thought weakly. Was he going to pay her off now? She trembled.

She had been too optimistic, she thought, imagining their relationship was permanent. Just because he'd said he loved her, she'd believed that it would last.

She hardly noticed the bedroom that had once inspired such delight in her. The marble floors, strewn with Chinese rugs, and the enormous four-poster bed. The windows stood wide to their own private balcony, where sometimes they had breakfast together. She could see that the maid had already delivered orange juice and coffee. The two jugs were standing on the white linen tablecloth that covered the table on the balcony, a basket of warm rolls and creamy butter just waiting for them to taste.

But Castelli didn't go out onto the balcony. Instead, he sat down on the side of the bed and gestured for her to sit beside him. Tess gathered the towel closer about her, feeling absurdly shy all of a sudden. If he was going to send her away, she thought, she didn't want any money from him.

'So,' he said at last, turning to look at her, and she had to force herself not to reach for him, to bestow a warm kiss on his lean, tanned cheek. There was a look of detachment in his eyes, a wary frown that defined her uncertainty. 'I have something to tell you,' he continued. 'I was going to tell you last night, but I—what do you say?—ducked out, yes? At the last minute.'

Tess was certain she knew what he was going to say now. The night before they'd had a romantic dinner together on the loggia, and afterwards they'd danced to the music from a trio of musicians who also worked on the estate. It had had all the makings of a special occasion—or a last evening, she acknowledged painfully. And instead of spoiling it by telling her their affair was over, he had taken her to bed and made frantic love to her for half the night.

Yes, she should definitely have realised that something was different, she thought despairingly. Would it make it easier for him if she told him she wanted to go? But no. She had to hear it from his lips. Even if it was the last thing he said to her. There must be no mistakes, no pre-emptive tears to make him change his mind.

Now she looked at him, keeping her tears at bay with an effort. 'Go on,' she said huskily. 'What is it you want to say?'

Castelli bent his head. 'It is not easy, Tess,' he said. 'You know I love you, do you not? Well, now I find that is not enough.'

'No?'

The word was barely audible, caught as it was by the tightness in her throat. 'No,' he said unevenly. 'I realise these weeks—months—together have been magical. But— I need more. I need to know you are mine. Not just physically but spiritually as well.'

Tess stared at him. 'I—I don't know what you mean,' she stammered.

'This is why I went down to the safe,' he said, producing a small box from beneath the satin coverlet of the bed. 'It is a ring, *cara*. It once belonged to my grandmother. I would like you to wear it. It is a betrothal ring, of course, and I know what that means.'

Tess swallowed. 'Does it mean you want to marry me?' she asked disbelievingly, and he nodded.

'But I will understand if you say no.' He caught her hand and took it to his lips. '*Cara*, I know we have never talked of marriage and it is a big step for you to take, but I would like you to consider it. You do not have to decide right away,' he added, seeing her stunned expression and misunderstanding its meaning. 'You can have all the time in the world.' His lips twitched. 'Well, the rest of the day, perhaps.'

'Oh, Rafe!' With a strangled cry she flung herself into his arms, laughing and crying together. 'I thought you were going to break up with me. I couldn't think of anything else you might want to say to me.'

'Break up with you?' He drew back to look into her face, and she saw his eyes were dark with emotion. 'I wanted to ask you to marry me weeks, no, months ago. But I wanted to give you time to be sure that this was what you really wanted, too.'

'Oh, Rafe!' She kissed him soundly and then drew back to let him put the ring on her finger. It fitted perfectly, and he gave a smug little grin.

'I had it sized,' he admitted, and she remembered how he had once pretended to admire her signet ring. 'So—will you marry me, *mi amore*? Will you live with me and be my love?'

And, of course, she said yes.

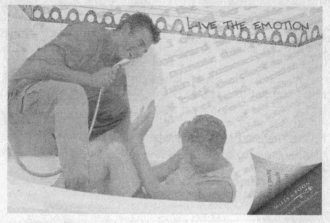

Modern
romance™

...international affairs
– seduction and
passion guaranteed

Medical
romance™

...pulse-raising
romance – heart-
racing medical drama

Tender
romance™

...sparkling, emotional,
feel-good romance

Sensual
romance™

...teasing, tempting,
provocatively playful

Historical
romance™

...rich, vivid and
passionate

Blaze™

...scorching hot
sexy reads

27 new titles every month.

Live the emotion

4 FREE

books and a surprise gift!

We would like to take this opportunity to thank you for reading this Mills & Boon® book by offering you the chance to take FOUR more specially selected titles from the Modern Romance™ series absolutely FREE! We're also making this offer to introduce you to the benefits of the Reader Service™—

- ★ FREE home delivery
- ★ FREE gifts and competitions
- ★ FREE monthly Newsletter
- ★ Exclusive Reader Service offers
- ★ Books available before they're in the shops

Accepting these FREE books and gift places you under no obligation to buy, you may cancel at any time, even after receiving your free shipment. Simply complete your details below and return the entire page to the address below. ***You don't even need a stamp!***

YES! Please send me 4 free Modern Romance books and a surprise gift. I understand that unless you hear from me, I will receive 6 superb new titles every month for just £2.69 each, postage and packing free. I am under no obligation to purchase any books and may cancel my subscription at any time. The free books and gift will be mine to keep in any case.

P4ZED

Ms/Mrs/Miss/Mr ....Initials..................................
                                                        BLOCK CAPITALS PLEASE

Surname ....

Address ....

....

....Postcode..............................

Send this whole page to:
UK: FREEPOST CN81, Croydon, CR9 3WZ
EIRE: PO Box 4546, Kilcock, County Kildare (stamp required)